1632 & Beyond Special Issue 2

1632 and Beyond, Iver P. Cooper, Edith Wild, Michael Lockwood, Jackie Britton-Lopatin, Marc Tyrell, Chuck Thompson, Mark Huston, John Deakins, Sarah Hays, George Haberberger, Eric Flint, Lucille Robbins, Walt Boyes, Bjorn Hasseler

Flint's Shards, Inc.

ERIC FLINT'S 1632 & BEYOND SPECIAL ISSUE #2

This is a work of fiction. Names, characters places, and events portrayed in this book are fictional or used fictitiously. Any resemblance to real people (living or dead), events, or places is coincidental.

Editor-in-Chief Bjorn Hasseler
Production and Design Bethanne Kim
Editor Chuck Thompson
Cover Artwork is a 1910 postcard by E.A. Schwerdtfeger & Co. from the New York Public Library, digitally enhanced by Raw Pixel.
Interior Art Garrett W. Vance

1. Science Fiction-Alternate History
2. Science Fiction-Time Travel

eBook ISBN: 978-1-962398-19-0
Paperback ISBN: 978-1-962398-20-6

Distributed by Flint's Shards Inc.
339 Heyward Street, #200
Columbia, SC 29201

Contents

Preface

In Fall 2021, Eric Flint and the staff of Ring of Fire Press decided to publish a Christmas anthology set in the 1632 universe. From the call for stories to publication was less than ninety days. Even with all their regular responsibilities (and day jobs!), the authors and editors managed it.

A 1632 Christmas contained 21 stories. To get them back in print, *Eric Flint's 1632 & Beyond* is issuing two bonus issues. The first contains nine of the stories, and the second contains eleven. The remaining story, David Carrico's "Canticle de Noel," will be included in the Baen reprint of *1635: Music & Murder* so that all the Marla & Franz stories are in one collection.

Happy reading!

Bjorn Hasseler

Bethanne Kim

Chuck Thompson

Introduction

When the up-timers arrived in the Germanies in 1631, they had to sort out many different issues. Some were economic. Some were political. Some were military. But above all, the up-timers and down-timers had to deal with the very real culture clash between the culture and mores of 2000 and those of 16 32.

Nowhere was the difference line so clear than in the ways Christmas was celebrated. They differed on the date that Santa Claus came, the identities of Santa's helpers, and even on whether Christmas should be celebrated at all.

In these stories, we see many different viewpoints as Christmas and the other holidays are celebrated across the New Time Line world. We have a Swedish Christmas in the Wonderland Isles, complete with dodos. We have a Swedish Christmas at home. We have a Japanese Christmas in what would have been California, and a Dutch Christmas in the new world. We have a young Jewish boy who has to learn about up-time Hanukkah traditions not yet created for the Jewish holiday. The Lapps find out that Santa is one of them, and Charles Dickens meets Kermit on a shaky and beat-up videotape. There are more, and we hope you enjoy them all.

This anthology is fondly dedicated to our friends, Rick Boatright, Kevin Evans and Karen Carnahan Evans, who have gone beyond but are never forgotten.

Walt Boyes

Bjorn Hasseler

Joy Ward

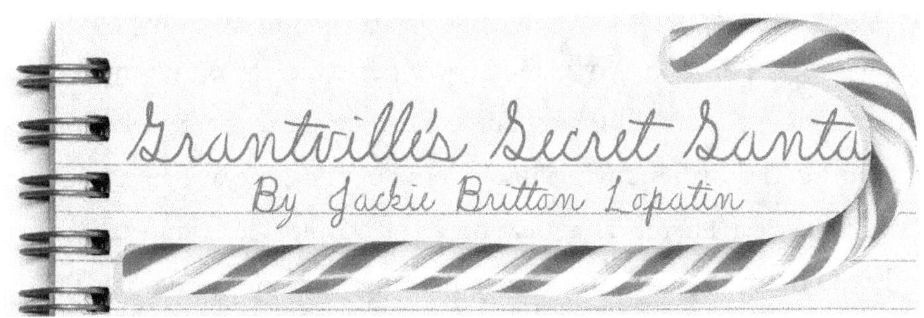

Grantville's Secret Santa

Jackie Britton-Lopatin

"Oh, I remember my first Grantville Christmas." The elderly woman spoke to her large audience from the podium. "It was amazing."

"I had recently started working part-time at the newspaper office so I was able to earn some rent money while learning more about journalism. The year was 1634, and I was just sixteen. I had been in Grantville for less than a year. My parents had brought me to Grantville the previous April to see if the up-time doctors could fix my leg. I had broken it when I was twelve, and although the break healed up fine, my unbroken leg had grown longer during what the doctors at the Leahy Center called a 'growth spurt' and I was left with two uneven legs. In my home village, that made me pretty much unemployable and unmarriageable, since who would marry a poor cripple? Wives needed two good legs to be able to get around as well as a good dowry. My sisters had been put out to service so that they could increase their dowries, but my parents spent what was supposed to be my dowry on this trip to Grantville in the hopes of giving me a more prosperous future.

"Grantville, though...oh, that was a revelation. So many possibilities we'd never considered for a girl like me...a little hampered in my mobility, but with a good brain. My parents were persuaded to enroll me for the summer semester at the high school so I could take the secretarial courses of typing and shorthand while undergoing physical therapy to strengthen my leg muscles. There was a great need for people who could take notes and type them up, and that was something that could be done sitting down. So although I would never be able to be put out to service as my sisters were, I would still become employable. The irony is that while my sisters were employed to mop floors and carry heavy jugs of water up and down stairs, I—the cripple—would end up being paid much better than them to sit in on all the best lectures at the high school and all the most important meetings at City Hall and to take notes. And I soaked up all that knowledge—as the Americans would say—like a sponge.

"The first journalism lecture I transcribed was eye-opening. I'd never really, really thought about the ethics of journalism before, and that there were different ways of reporting facts to influence the ways people think. I learned about 'yellow journalism' and how to recognize it. I also was able to look at the many wonders of Grantville and put down the facts and my feelings about them simply and clearly. My very first sale was a paper I wrote for an English writing class about the many gifts of Grantville. That simple piece—which sold to newspapers all over the Germanies and paid me enough to continue my studies up at the high school—convinced Paul Kindred to hire me part-time and continue my training as a reporter. I started as a simple transcriber of facts and progressed through his tutelage into my successful career as a journalist and writer. He taught me not just how to report on the facts, but how to take those same facts and get many different types of stories out of them, creating multiple income streams out of one lecture or experience. I was only just beginning those lessons when I learned about the American custom of "the Secret Santa."

The woman smiled at the memories and her audience faded away as she began her recounting of the events she had experienced in her youth.

"We'd been talking up the Christmas season at the newspaper office since early November, well before the American Thanksgiving. The advertising salespeople explained "Black Friday" to everyone who would listen, all in a very American way of selling advertising. At home we had celebrated a simple Christmas, hanging greens, going to church and eating a good dinner. Not feasting and drinking in the ways of some households, and we were not wealthy enough to have a big *Tannenbaum* in our household, but not so very different from the American Christmas celebrations. Mr. Kindred encouraged me to research American Christmas customs and write an article on what I found and how it compared to my village.

"What I found was Americans had—in their way—taken the celebrations brought to them by their German and English immigrants and expanded on them. We decorated our houses and trees with candles and homemade garlands and ornaments? They devoted whole industries to producing elaborate ornamentations and strings of electric lights. We exchanged simple gifts with family members? They exchanged elaborately wrapped gifts not just with their immediate family but with many of their friends. Each of our households had a family feast? Americans had such a surplus of wealth that they shared their feasting in the form of 'goodie boxes' filled with all manner of homemade cookies and candies.

"I was overwhelmed with all the information I found at the public library and learned from talking with friends and co-workers. It seems that in the America the up-timers came from, almost every year had brought at least one wonderful new story, custom, or song for Christmas, each of them special in its own particular way. It was, indeed, considered the most wonderful time of the year, and a white Christmas was to be prized above all. These Christmas customs and songs ranged from the enormously silly—but fun!—to the amazingly holy and uplifting. The radio stations were able to fill our airways with joyous holiday melodies, and the video station had to carefully coordinate their Christmas presentations with the different church schedules so that there was a minimum amount of competition for people's attention. The churches would have been quite distressed if too many people were staying home to watch a Christmas movie on the evenings when it was time for their choirs to practice their Christmas music, and while the businesses were happy to have carolers come around and sing during the daylight hours, they preferred to have the *kinder* stay away in the mornings, so this was when some of the children's programming was aired on the television sets. Americans just loved their Christmas programming, and I found it astonishing just how many of the up-timers had not only commercially prepared copies of their favorite shows, but had videotaped local performances starring their children and grandchildren. It seemed that all of the school systems, from preschools through high school had had their seasonal celebrations and parties. The sharing of home recordings of Christmas parades by the high school's video department spawned a whole industry of clowns as newcomers to Grantville wanted ways of meeting and talking with up-timers beyond joining a church or taking classes. The clowns really came into their own during the Fourth of July parades, but they took their inspiration from Christmas parade videos.

Shaking her head, she smiled ruefully at her audience.

"I was quite distressed at first to learn that adults were expected to exchange gifts on an equal basis with other adults as well as provide gifts for all the *kinder* in your family, and then relieved to find that children and students weren't held to the same adult standards. I also found that the group of adults in our newspaper office would be putting their names into a hat to be drawn out by their 'Secret Santa.' It was explained to me as a fun way to celebrate the season while keeping the costs down. Trying to buy even small gifts for all of your co-workers could add up to quite a lot of money during an already expensive season, but by drawing names and putting a price limit on what you could spend on the gifts made the gift giving both manageable and fun. At least it seemed that way to the up-timers."

She paused in her narration to take a sip of water.

"Once I learned that I wasn't expected to either bake goodies for everybody or figure out more than one gift for the people in the newspaper office, I was mostly able to relax and marvel at the season. As I reported on the various Christmas celebrations being planned around town, Mr. Kindred credited me with pointing out just how over-the-top and competitive each group was being. One church had a nativity scene? Another church wanted to have a live nativity scene complete with sheep, shepherds, wise men, and choirs of angels. Christmas bazaars were held as fund-raisers for different churches and non-profit groups and I was very glad that my press credentials got me invited to see many of the displays before the general public was let in. That's how I was able to find most of the gifts I gave that year. Little things, but funny or useful. I also got a good taste of the holiday season, and it was yummy!

"One of the first Christmas articles with my byline led to a holiday cookbook being produced as a fundraiser for the joint council of Grantville churches. Up-timers definitely took their notions of fun seriously, and I found it amazing how many out-of-the-ordinary ingredients they used in their holiday cooking. Chocolate chips. Colored sprinkles. Marshmallows. Puffed rice. Rolled oats...not just regular oats that we fed to horses or made into porridge, but rolled oats. Cocoa powder. Sugar powder. Colored sugar crystals. Concentrated food dyes so that they could make colored icing for their sugar cookies. The first Christmas they celebrated in 1631 was very pitiful by their standards, but by 1634 they had very definite ideas of what their Christmas celebrations should include, and whole industries were created to satisfy them. Each ingredient warranted its own story when it was produced, but none more so than the first batch of vanilla extract. If the Nasi family connections hadn't been able to import both vanilla and cacao beans as well as the always necessary coffee beans through their contacts, I swear there were women in Grantville who would have set sail to Mexico to find them for themselves. The cost didn't matter because Christmas wouldn't be the same without them. Christmas without chocolate or sugar cookies? Unthinkable!

"But back to the Secret Santa.

"I learned that there are many ways to conduct a Secret Santa exchange. One co-worker described how her dorm floor in college did it, which was to leave their Secret Santa a candy cane or chocolate bar or other trifle each day for a week before classes were over and their holidays began. Another told about how each of the participants were to bring a wrapped gift in the designated price range to the office party, and those who brought a gift got a gift, so nobody was forced to participate but nobody who participated was left without a gift. That sounded best to us, so that's the way we did it. I found hand-woven baskets at one church bazaar and some of the newest soaps made from up-time recipes at another and combined them with colorful ribbons from the Lothlorien Dye Works to make very attractive gift baskets...one for my secret Santa and several for other friends I'd made at my rooming house. The party at the newspaper office was held the Thursday before Christmas, right after the latest issue had been put to bed. That issue was delivered that Sunday, which happened to be Christmas Eve. It was, as always, filled with news and lots and lots of advertisements, but it also included some particularly poignant or iconic Christmas features. The editorial page printed the ever popular "Yes, Virginia, there is a Santa Claus," and the entire "Visit from Saint Nicholas" poem by Clement Moore was printed on the front page. The back page, which was usually taken up by advertisements—very expensive advertisements—was devoted to the Christmas Caroling sponsored by the Joint Churches of Grantville and included the lyrics of a great many of the most popular carols.

"Those gifts made me feel good, but I was quickly figuring out that the true value of my stay in Grantville wasn't in the *things* that I was seeing and accumulating, but the *ideas* and *lessons* I was learning. I wanted to share these with my home village, and I wasn't sure what was practical...or legal. Mr. Kindred had negotiated the rights for me to use information I learned from the lectures I transcribed in my articles and other writings, but the actual lectures themselves belonged to the teachers who gave them. It was up to them to have them published or not, and I couldn't just transcribe my notes and give copies as gifts. *I* was getting a world class education and learning skills that would help me all my life, but I didn't have the right to plagiarize these lectures wholesale because the giving of lectures—or writing of books on these topics—were these teachers' livelihoods. If I betrayed any of these teachers' trust, they would stop calling on me to transcribe their lectures and the question-and-answer sessions which followed them, and that would definitely damage my income. Ethics, I was learning, weren't just there for godly reasons, but for good *practical* reasons. If your ethics were too flexible, nobody could trust you or would hire you. But I still wanted to find some way of sharing the information I learned. So I did the only thing I could think of...I talked with my co-worker and friend Betsy Springer.

I showed Betsy my ring binder notebook filled with all the lectures I'd transcribed that year and explained how I wanted to share some of the lectures with my sisters for Christmas, but that ethics were preventing me from doing so. She's the one who suggested to Mr. Kindred that it might be good to contact all the region's transcriptionists and produce a 'highlights of the educational year in review' for the post-Christmas/pre-New Year's issue. A way to increase sales for this issue and promote Grantville's whole lecture industry. A few of Grantville's teachers had stopped being what the up-timers thought of as 'regular' teachers and had begun concentrating on their particular specialties, creating lecture series that they could be hired to give. Others rotated through schools throughout West Virginia County. As the railroad system expanded, the lecture circuit expanded accordingly.

Not surprisingly, the educational review article was a big success for newspapers all over the Germanies, the lecture circuit, and all of us who were hired to transcribe individual lectures. Books were published on the strength of this annual column, and many teachers became famous. In the meantime, once the railroad system had been expanded to my home village, I was finally able to join the lecture circuit myself. I talked about Grantville and journalism and shared my knowledge of shorthand with many young people...including my sisters.

And so that's how my first American Christmas changed not just my life but my whole family's life. My sisters didn't become journalists, but the skills they learned brought them much more money than hauling buckets of water and mopping floors ever could, and they were able to make much better marriages sooner than they expected. Me? I'd been totally spoiled by the luxuries and ideals of Grantville. I liked the people I met, and I enjoyed writing about what I learned along the way. That I was able to earn good money from my writing was definitely a plus, but most of all I came to be enchanted with the notion of contributing to a better future. A future in which the America which produced the Grantville I loved was possible. I've traveled as far and wide as the up-time-based railroad could take me, but when it came time to retire, it was Grantville I chose as my home. I have everything I need within walking distance of my small apartment...the high school with its research library, shopping, good friends and neighbors, and a never-ending stream of interesting visitors to interview, uh," she looked a little embarrassed at her slip of the tongue, "I mean talk with. The Leahy Medical Center is just a short drive away and assisted living homes are there for when I need them. And in Grantville, Christmas truly is the best time of the year."

The Gift

Chuck Thompson

Grantville

December, 1636

Most mornings, before rising, Inez Wiley liked to warm her brain by going over her plans for the next few days. She had gotten halfway through tomorrow when a sound interrupted her thoughts. *Skritch skritch. Skritch skritch.* "Better be that tabby alley cat scratching at my door and not some red-headed goblin-girl named Anna trying to get me up early."

Inez smiled at the sound of tiptoed pattering in the hallway and a muffled giggle that drifted back toward her. She swung her feet over the bed, into threadbare slippers, and gave the air a sniff. "Umm. Nothing like getting up to the smell of coffee." She knew that Anna's mother, Erna Wolrad, was downstairs brewing it just for her. Neither Erna, nor her husband Jobst, cared for coffee.

And then Inez remembered and frowned. Jobst was taking part of today off to look for a place of their own to rent. He said he was grateful for

Inez taking them in when they had no place else to go, but he could not impose any longer. It was not proper. His carpentry business did well now. They could afford a house and, therefore, they should not lean on the kindness of others. Inez could not get him to understand that she wasn't an *other*. She had fallen in love with her little refugee family. The Wolrads had filled a hole in her heart. The Ring of Fire that had brought a piece of West Virginia to 1631 Germany had made that hole. It separated her from most of her children who were outside the Ring when it hit. After they got here, Enoch was killed. God had brought the Wolrads to her and they were meant to stay together. *I must convince him somehow.*

Inez came downstairs and walked into the kitchen. Anna was sitting at the kitchen table, her legs swinging. Such a bright girl, and she had spunk that would make Pippi Longstocking seem elderly. Anna resembled Pippi in other ways, with long red hair, and a slim tallness she would appreciate when she got older. For now, Inez knew she didn't much like looking down on her classmates or the teasing from some of the boys. Inez crooked a finger at her and squished her face. This earned her a laugh, and Anna jumped off the chair and rushed over to give Inez a hug.

Erna turned around from the stove. "And what are you two up to already with the giggling and hugging?"

Anna looked up at Inez and opened her eyes wide and cocked her head a little.

Inez knew that look. *Don't tell, please.* "Yes," Inez said, "nothing to see here."

"Hmm. Well. I know better than to ask you two conspirators." Erna smiled at Inez and her hand dropped to the top of her prominent belly and rested there. Erna was a petite and pretty woman and about the most down-to-earth person Inez had ever met. *Fortune smiled on me the day I first saw her*, Jobst liked to say.

Inez walked and placed her own hand on top of Erna's. "A boy, I think. I usually get it right." Inez gave her a small hug. "What's left for breakfast for lazy late sleepers like me?"

"Today we have a lovely up-timer omelet. With cheese and ham." Erna turned back to the stove and waggled her spatula at Anna. "And something tells me you might have tarried a little longer."

Anna's mouth dropped open.

"Ha! You see Anna. You can't get anything by your mother."

A rapping on the back door interrupted them. As they looked, Gina Wiley opened the door and came in. Gina was now Inez's daughter-in-law. For the second time. Hopefully, her son Will would not screw it up again. The original wild man. He did seem to be controlling himself better since Enoch's death. Under Gina's arm, she had a grapevine basket and Inez knew what it contained. Cinnamon rolls. Gina made the best.

"Aunt Gina," Anna said. "Is Brette coming too?"

"I'm sorry sweetie, but no. She's at basketball practice. But she wanted me to ask if you and Gammy are going to the movies this afternoon. She wants to meet you there."

"Are we Gammy?"

"Well," Inez said. "I suppose I might be persuaded."

Gina winked at Inez and turned to Erna. She hugged her and then gave her belly a poke. "Well, you're about to explode. Sure there aren't two in there?"

"The doctor says one. And Inez agrees. And Inez has midwifed more babies into this world than the doctor has seen in. If they both say so, it must be true."

"Gina," Inez said. "I've seen smaller grins on a briar-eating mule. And you're practically dancing. What gives?"

Gina blushed. "Nothing. Let's get out these buns, and I need a cup of coffee." Gina turned away from Inez and started examining her basket.

Inez cocked her head at Gina and her left eye squinched in a bit. She got up from her chair and walked over and, with one hand on Gina's shoulder, gently pulled her around so they faced one another.

Gina wouldn't look her in the eye, but Inez could see a slip of a smile on her face. Inez tilted her chin up and gave her a close look, toe to head.

"Gina Wiley. Are you cookin' me a grandbaby?"

At that, Gina's eyes watered and her grin widened. "Yeah, Inez. I reckon I am."

Inez pulled her into a tight hug. Erna rushed over and joined them.

"Hey. What's going on," Anna said. "What's wrong?"

Inez let go of the two women and kneeled to Anna's level. "Nothing, dear child. Your Aunt Gina is going to have a baby too."

"Wow. Neat. Mom's baby and Aunt Gina's can be good friends like Brette and me, right?"

"I am sure of it," Inez said.

Erna and Gina were still holding each other. "I am so happy, Gina," Erna said. "God has blessed us mightily." Erna looked over to Inez and held out her hand to her. Inez took it. "Thank you, dear Lord, for this blessing and for this family. I do not know what we would have done had we not found you. This time two years ago, Jobst, Anna, and I were hungry, homeless, and the cruel war had taken all our family. God's grace brought us to this place and to you."

"Oh, Erna. It is you and your family who have helped heal us. I love you all so much," Inez said.

Just at that moment, Jobst walked into the house. Inez noticed him standing in the kitchen doorway, like a deer in the headlights. His wide eyes darted from one woman to the next and back again. "*Was ist*...um, what is wrong? What has happened? Is this about moving out again?"

Erna pulled the bottom of her cooking apron up and dabbed her eyes dry. She walked over to Jobst and stood on her tiptoes and kissed him. "No, foolish man. Our dear Gina is with child."

Jobst relaxed and let out the breath he had been holding. "Ah. I see. Congratulations. And why are we crying?"

"Pfft! Why do you ask. Just sit and I will bring you some water and warm one of Gina's delicious pastries for you. How went the house hunting? We don't usually see you mid-morning."

With that, Jobst sat down and shook his head. "Not well I am afraid. Demand is quite high. I was just around the corner, so I thought I would stop in. There is nothing near town within our means. I will have to look further away. Much further."

Anna's face fell. "Oh no Papa. We must be close to Gammy and Brette and Aunt Gina. I don't want to go live far away!"

"Anna. I have tried to explain, and you will understand when you get older. It is not right to live in someone else's house who is not your family. Not when you can afford to stand on your own two feet. Don't you want your own place?"

"No! I don't. She is family. She is *my* Gammy!" And, with that, she ran out of the kitchen, unsuccessfully trying to suppress a cry. Inez heard her go up the stairs and close the door to her room. Jobst made a move to go after her but stayed at Erna's touch on his arm.

"Let her be for a while. I'll go talk to her later."

Inez shifted in her chair and looked over at Jobst. "Jobst. You know you can just—"

"No, Frau Wiley. Please, let us not discuss that again. As much as we care for you and your family, it is not fitting we stay here any longer."

"Well, pay me rent if that makes you feel better."

"That will not do either. I know what this house is worth in rent and that amount is out of the question. I would pay no less. And people would still think I am not standing on my own. I cannot. And that is my final word on this please."

Inez decided to let it go. Even the *Frau* part. For now.

* * *

The next day, the skies shone bright with promise. A beautiful Sunday. After church, Inez had promised to take Anna downtown to see the Christmas decorations and all the shop windows. An impromptu competition had begun among the merchants for the best displays. Roth Jewelers supposedly had an elaborate animated display of Santa on his sleigh. Anna bounced with excitement and could not wait for lunch to be over so they could head out. Jobst usually spent Sunday afternoon planning the activities on his job sites. He had ten employees now and was stretched thin trying to keep all the general contractors happy. But Anna's exuberance was irresistible. Inez knew that Jobst's world revolved around his girls. He never missed the chance for a joyful outing with them.

What a glorious day. Chilly. But if you turned your back to the sun, it felt like you were standing in front of a cozy wood stove. Though the shops were almost all closed, there were quite a few people walking around, also window gazing. The town set up a very large Christmas tree in the middle of downtown. The school children had made hundreds of little paper white angels and the town completed the look with white electric lights, some kind of fake snow, and silver tinsel garlands. Anna walked round and round it until her neck got sore from looking up.

"Isn't it beautiful, Papa?"

Jobst leaned down to her. "It is, my sweet. Maybe we can have our own tree in our own house by Christmas?"

Anna pulled in her lower lip and frowned. She opened her mouth to speak, but then must have decided better of it. Instead, she grabbed Jobst's hand. "Come on, Papa. I want to go see the moving Santa next."

Jobst smiled and allowed himself to be pulled along. Inez and Erna followed, their arms intertwined, like old school friends. Erna leaned her cheek into Inez's for a moment and gave her arm a squeeze.

Anna stared in wonder at the Santa display, as did Erna and Jobst. Inez smiled in amusement. The Santa rocked back and forth in his sleigh and waved at them. His little black pipe emitted a puff of smoke several times every minute. The model-maker suspended the sleigh above a diorama of Grantville, as if St. Nick flew overhead. Tiny little people looked up from below. The reindeer bobbed back and forth and their legs moved in a cantering rhythm. Anna inspected the display from every angle and even demanded that Jobst put her on his shoulders so she could see it from above.

"How does it work?"

Jobst smiled. "Well, much like Frau, er, Ms. Inez's cuckoo clock in the living room. But more complicated."

"Will you draw it for me Papa? The insides I mean. I want to know."

Jobst laughed. "I will try, sweetling. When we get home. Now. I noticed a street cart with hot apple cider and another with popcorn. What do you say we spend a little on some treats?"

"Oh yes! Thank you, Papa. Can I buy Gammy's for her?"

"Of course. You are so kind. How God has blessed me with such a caring daughter."

Anna blushed and grinned. She ran back to Inez and grabbed her hand. "Come on, Gammy. Let's go!"

As they walked to where the street carts were, Inez caught something out of the corner of her eye and turned to look. She had not noticed that a law firm had a statue of lady justice outside their front door.

Anna followed Inez's gaze. "What's that? Is it for Christmas? Why is she blindfolded and holding a sword?"

"No. Not for Christmas. That is lady justice. She represents the legal system. The blindfold shows that she does not care whether you are poor or rich. The scales mean she will weigh each person's side of the story fairly, and the sword tells us that she will deliver justice to those who need it."

"Why is she outside a shop?"

"Not a shop, Anna. Lady justice there means that place is where men and women called lawyers help people with legal matters. That means they help them resolve disputes peacefully, or defend someone who is arrested, or they create documents that record important transactions."

Anna frowned. "What are tran-actions."

"Transactions. They are like...well, say I sold my house. We need something on paper that shows I sold it to someone else so they can show everyone that, yes, this is now my house, and I can prove it." Inez regretted that example almost immediately. But it popped into her mind because her house, and who lived there, was always on her mind.

They started walking again. Just loud enough for Inez to hear, Anna whispered: "I don't want to leave your house ever. Why does Papa want to move away? It's a terrible, awful, stinky idea."

Inez squeezed her hand. "Your Papa is doing what he thinks is best. We can talk about it later, and I will try to explain. Now. What are you going to get on your popcorn?"

The rest of the day, Inez thought about that statue. It gave her a little seed of an idea. And the next morning, attorney Laura Koudsi had an unexpected visitor waiting for her.

"Ms. Inez. What a surprise. Do you need help? I don't really have any open—"

"I do apologize. I will not need an appointment yet. I don't think I even need to come inside. I need to know if something is possible. Of course, I would insist on paying a retainer or whatever is required."

Laura pulled her keys out. "Well. Let's go inside anyway and be warm. I can spare a few moments. But I have to get ready for a hearing, so it will need to be quick."

* * *

A week later, Inez had what she wanted. A legal petition. She showed it to Erna the first quiet moment she could.

Erna sat at the kitchen table with her tea growing cold and asked Inez to explain it one more time. Inez felt a tough knot in her stomach. She really wasn't sure how Erna would take her proposal. She might be mad. Offended. And then Inez saw she wasn't those things at all. Erna's hands went to her face and she bowed her head. After a moment, she wiped away the moisture.

"It is a beautiful thing to offer, dearest Inez. It would be my honor to accept. We must, of course, ask Jobst."

"I was worried you might be upset about this idea. That it might look like I was asking you to forget your family that is gone."

"Oh no. It is lovely beyond words. It will not make me cherish my own any less."

"I have a plan. We will make Jobst that schnitzel he likes so very much. I picked up some veal this morning. With the anchovy paste. It's Friday, and he'll have an after-dinner scotch and water. That should help grease the skids. What do you think?"

Erna frowned. "This seems, what is your word? Sneaky."

"Only a little, my dear. And we are going to tell him everything so, really, not even that."

Erna looked down. "He has too much of his father in him. Herr Wolrad was a fair man and respectful. But stern and always very proper. And no one would say he was loving. Jobst absorbed much of that I am afraid."

Inez leaned over. "But Jobst is certainly not unloving. He dotes on you and Anna. And, unlike many Germans I have met, he is not shy about telling you of his love."

Erna blushed. "This is true. I would not have married a man like his father. But saying yes to Jobst was as easy as falling into a pond."

Inez smiled. "Well, we had best get to work."

That evening, they were just getting finished, when Inez heard Jobst come in.

"Oho! Do I smell schnitzel? A fine end to a fine day."

Jobst entered the kitchen. "I got two new jobs today. I thought nothing would make me feel better. Wonderful indeed." Jobst actually slapped his hands together and rubbed them. He reached out for the oven door where Inez had placed the schnitzel to keep warm. Inez reached over with her wooden spoon and smacked him on the knuckles.

He laughed. "Ouch. You witch. I will call the Krampus to come chop you up."

"Good. And then he can cook your schnitzel for you. No samples for you. Go get washed, and it will be all on the table when you get back."

Jobst laughed again on the way to the bathroom.

After dinner, Jobst gladly accepted the offered scotch. Inez poured herself a finger and sat across the table from him. She had just sent Anna upstairs to find a new pack of crayons Inez had bought a few days ago. Those things were getting pricey.

"Jobst, I have some things I would like to talk to you about. Erna and I."

Jobst lowered his glass to the table and let out a sigh. "I supposed I knew this was all too good to be true. Oh, well. You have earned my polite attention to your latest scheme."

Jobst smiled, but Inez wondered how long that might last. She cleared her throat. "As you know. I love you all as dearly as my own children. I have had my own losses, as have you and Erna. I can never replace your parents and family who are gone but, as much as I can, I would like to stand in their stead. Though I believe no paper could bind us together more tightly, I would like to formally, legally, adopt Erna as my own child. I have already discussed it with a lawyer, and she assures me it can be done. Erna would be my own, by love and by law. With your agreement, of course."

To his credit, though the smile disappeared, Jobst paused a long while before answering. "I do not know. I have heard of the nobility doing such things but...I just do not know. I am not sure...."

"There is more. Erna would be my child in all respects. With right of inheritance. No one can say it is not proper that we live together as family now—"

Now Jobst frowned. "Ah. I see what this is. I do not think this makes anything more proper—"

Erna stood. "Jobst Wolrad! You are not your father. I know you love me. You love Anna. And I know you love Inez as much as you ever cared for any of your blood. We are already family and always will be. If this piece of paper makes it easier for anyone, including you, to accept, then good. But I don't think you needed anything more than what was already in your heart. If you must bury some of your pride then I say good riddance, and I will be the first to scatter the earth on top of it—"

Erna broke off and looked toward the hall door. Inez and Jobst turned to see what she was looking at. Anna stood in the doorway.

Her lip quivered. "Does this mean I can have a real Gammy? Kids at school say she isn't my real Gammy, and I can't call her that. But I do anyway. Please Papa. Can we make her my real Gammy?"

Inez walked over to Anna and knelt down. She held her by the shoulders and pulled her in. "I will always be your Gammy. Longer than the moon and stars are in the sky."

Erna raised her hand to her face and started to cry. With her other hand, she grabbed Jobst's shoulder and sank into his lap and wrapped both arms around him. Her tears began to fall on his shirt, wetting it.

Jobst looked at Anna and Inez, still holding one another. He stroked Erna's hair. "Forgive me. I have been a very foolish man. Yes. Of course. This would make me very happy. What a wonderful Christmas present."

At Christmas Time

Mark Huston

Based on the Anton Chekov story

"What shall I write, old woman?"

"A letter to my daughter. And her husband," replied Hilde. They were sitting in the smoky common room of the village inn. "For Christmas," she added with a stiff nod to the young man who sat across from her. She looked over her shoulder at her husband, standing behind. His eyes were beginning to cloud with cataracts, and he held his hat in his hard hands, ever so gently. He looked off into the distance, distracted and quiet.

Their daughter, Gisela, had moved away three and a half years ago. She married a man from Baden, a Catholic, and he had taken her there. He was a soldier, retired from the Catholic armies. Hilde and her husband didn't like him, but what could be done? In those times, before the Ring of Fire, with so few young men in their small village, so much war, a suitor that would take her from their home was the best thing for their daughter. In the first year they received one letter, and nothing after that. Three and a half years of silence.

They had nearly starved to death after Tilly's army came through, but the up-timers helped them to survive. Hilde believed the up-timers were sent from God; why else would they be here? Without them they surely would have died, and who knows what would have happened to Gisela. No, it was better that she was in Baden, far away from Thuringia, safe. She prayed it was so, and her heart ached at the absence.

The room was hot, too warm. She was used to her cool home, and this heat made her eyes swim.

"And my payment? Do you have it?"

She squinted at the young man, a student from the nearby town of Jena. Sparse beard, unruly dark hair, a boy of squandered privilege. A future he was likely to waste. Regarding him with thinly veiled disdain, she reached into her purse. She pulled out two coins and snapped them down on the table. Her gnarled fingers still gripped like iron, as milking goats and mucking stalls were needed every day.

"That is only half, old woman."

"When you are finished, I will give you the rest, if I am satisfied." Hilde was not one to part with any coin, no matter how small. Frivolity was not in her nature. Life was hard.

"If you cannot read or write, how will you know if you are satisfied or not?"

She squinted at him again, holding her purse in front of her with both hands. "I will know, young man."

He shook his head. "That is not the way I usually do this."

She reached out for the coins and began to put them into her purse.

"Wait!" the student said. They both gazed at each other. After a moment, he sighed heavily. "I can make an exception for you."

She sniffed, not wanting to overplay her hand. This letter was important. Her heart hurt. It must be sent. But coin is coin. She slowly set the money back on the table. "Very well," she said. "Half now, and half when complete."

The student nodded, managing a half smile. "So, what shall I write, old woman?"

She gave the student her daughter's address. They lived in a new spa that was in the town of Baden-Baden. Her husband was a doorman there, his old commander the owner. His old commander was from the town and held the favor of the margrave. The up-time Baden-Baden was known for its spring water, and the commander read from the Grantville library about the spas that were built there in the nineteenth century. He wanted to build the first one, and he had taken Gisela's husband, Ernst, with him to operate it. Hilde knew they were Catholic there, which always left a knot in her stomach.

The student read the address back to her. "Now what do you wish me to write, old woman?" His pen was poised over the inkwell. He was using one of the fancy up-time-designed nib pens. She saw his eyes catch her looking at the delicate metal pen tip. He smiled and gave her a little fake shrug. "If one is to write, one needs good tools. Nobody uses quill anymore if one can help it."

She tried to focus, and took a breath of the too warm air, thick with odors of food and people. "To our dear son-in-law, Ernst Koch, and our daughter, Gisela Wagner, we send you greetings at this time of our Savior's birth and pray that this finds you well and whole." She paused, and then started to cry. The heat in the room, the smug young man, and the pain of the aching unknown caused her to sob. She felt her husband's hand on her shoulder, and she turned to him, hopeful.

His gaze was still distant, but he shifted it to her. "It is warm here."

She stifled another sob. "Yes. Very warm."

"Are we done?" He moved to put his hat back on, gaze slowly shifting away.

"No, Hans. We are not done. I must write to Gisela."

He took his hat off, and continued his gaze, now focused on the hearthstone with its blazing fire below.

Hilde turned back to the young man, and her mind went blank. While lying awake at night, there were so many things she wanted to say, so many things to tell Gisela about in the village. Old Uncle Johann and his passing, God bless his soul. The need in the selling of the cow. New goats. Her father, who was fading like an ember carried aloft in the smoke. So many things. The up-timers and their equipment, the radio in the village, new people, the carriages that moved as if by magic. The hunger, so much hunger. Not this year, thank the Lord. But the heat, the sorrow, the confusion, they all conspired to freeze her mind.

She blinked at the student as her vision blurred. "I—I don't know. I..." Her hand reached for the coins on the table, almost involuntarily. She moved slowly. The student swiped them up, and her fingers closed on empty space.

"This is a good beginning," he said. He showed her the paper, scrolling whorls and elegant squiggles across the top of the page. It looked elegant. "If you do not know what to write, I can do it for you. What does your son-in-law do?"

Her tears streamed down her face, slower now. She saw the proprietor of the inn look at her with concern, and she turned away, ashamed. Still her mind was blank. "He is a doorman at a spa. He was a soldier, but he has retired." Her voice sounded desperate.

The student nodded. His face was flushed and fleshy, his fingers stubby and fat. His fingernails were stained with ink, and small spectacles gave him a piggy-like countenance. Sweat beaded on his forehead. "A retired soldier?" he asked. She nodded and placed her hand upon her husband's on her shoulder. "I have studied the soldier's laws and regulations. I can write about those." He proceeded to attack the page, writing quickly and smoothly, only pausing to add ink to his nib from the inkwell. "You have paid for the pages, old woman, I shall fill them." And he did. "The ranks of the soldier start at a private, and go up to the level of a general...all soldiers must obey orders from their superior officer...a regiment can be commanded by a general or a colonel...the standard infantry formation is a tercio, derived from the Spanish and used..." he droned on, filling the pages agreed upon with fine letters.

After a moment, he turned the agreed upon pages to her. She looked at them, and nodded. "That is pretty." She was astounded that such craftsmanship could be produced by such a selfish man.

"So, do I get my other half, old woman? I say, can I get my other half of the money?" He waved the letter in front of her face, rudely, to get her attention. It was so warm there.

Mechanically, she reached into her small purse, and pulled out the last two coins. He had, after all, done what she asked. She placed them on the table, this time with a gentler motion. He folded the letter with precision and handed it to her.

"You will have to mail it from Jena, there is a new post office there. They will tell you what it will cost. You should seal it with wax." He pointed to the folded paper. "Here."

She felt herself nod to him, and almost in a dream, took the paper and stood.

Her husband's gaze returned to her from the fireplace. "Is it time to go home?"

"Yes," she replied.

They made their way out of the inn and began the long walk home. The cold December air was like a slap in the face, waking her from her trance. A stray dog approached them, looking for a handout, and she swiped at it with her walking stick.

She missed, the dog being used to such things.

* * *

Ernst Koch looked at the letter and recognized it as from the little village in Thuringia. For now, he placed it in his pocket. He would give it to her later after he read it. For now, he had to do his duty as the bell for the front door was jangling. It was ten in the morning, as he could tell from the church bells sounding the hour. It was time for the old general to arrive for his baths.

"Good morning to you, sir, and a happy new year to you!" Ernst's voice was chipper, his face warm and welcoming. Every inch a picture of perfection.

The old general huffed at him in his normal confused manner. "Yes, and to you too Ernst. Happy New Year. At least we are able to keep our Julian calendar here, and not that one from the infernal up-timers." He was a pale large man, well into his seventies, and moved with a marked limp, the result of a fall from a horse while in the army. He looked even paler today. Ernst was far too circumspect to tell the man he was wrong about the calendars. He was once a general, after all.

"A very good thing, sir." He bowed slightly, showing great deference. "Are you here for your hydrotherapeutic bath today?"

"What?" He looked confused for a moment. Then he looked around at his surroundings. "Why else would I be at the spa?"

"Right this way, sir. The heated baths are on the upper floor." With that, Ernst escorted the man to the attendants waiting on the next level, returned to his station, and began to read the newspaper. He would look at the letter later. Whatever was in it was of no concern.

A few customers came and went. Ernst showed proper respect to all according to their station, and hid any hint of resentment when that same respect was not returned. His desire was to flail those who disrespected him with his fists and a cudgel he kept under his jacket. But he smiled nonetheless. He could do no more.

He went to the lower level of the spa where his apartment was allowed. His old commander had provided it as a place for a doorman. Ernst had earned the position when he and his commander served with General Hoch. He pushed the door open, and saw his wife sitting on the edge of the bed, the baby in her arms. The oldest boy was on the floor in front of her, and the middle was asleep behind her.

Her head turned to him as the door squeaked on its hinges, and her eyes at first showed fear as they evaluated his mood, and then relief, and then after a pause, she smiled. Ernst did not believe in the smile, but he knew the fear to be true. She did fear him.

"The general came today." His voice was flat.

She replied to him in a near whisper, not wanting to wake the children. Ernst did not like noisy children. They were an irritation, so Gisela always did her best to keep them quiet. She feared the consequences of his unhappiness. "The general! Did he remember you today?" she asked.

He shrugged with a noncommittal roll of his head. "He sometimes forgets to tip me." That caused him to pat his jacket pockets; there was something that he was forgetting. His fingers found the letter. It was good that she reminded him. She sent several letters to that stupid village he had rescued her from, and Ernst would carry them around in his jacket pocket until he forgot about them. Then he would throw them away.

He held it out in front of him.

She looked puzzled at first, then saw what it was. With the babe in her arms, she rose to take it from him. She moved like a frightened doe at twilight, tentative, afraid of closing the open distance, afraid of what she might find when she arrived. He placed the letter in her hands. She took it, reading the cover and looked at the broken wax seal. "It is from my village!" she said in a near whisper.

"I read it. It is a strange letter. It starts well enough, but it goes on about military things for the rest of the pages. It is mostly to me, I suppose." He felt this was natural enough, although he could not quite grasp why.

She inched backwards to the bed, not turning her back to him. "Thank you, Ernst." She sat, and then placed the baby on the bed next to her sleeping brother. She unfolded the wrinkled paper and began to read. "To our dear son-in-law, Ernst Koch, and our daughter, Gise..." Her voice trailed off, and then she began to sob. The oldest stood and went to his mother from the floor; he knew this meant she was sad. She gasped for a few moments, catching her sobs. She continued. "...we send you greetings at this time of our Savior's birth, and pray that this finds you well and whole." She caught her sobs and looked at the little boy, named Johann after the commander. The other boy stood sleepily and leaned against her mother. "It is from my mother and father. After so many years!" She turned to the children, excitement in her voice. "It is from your Opa and Oma!"

She continued to read, a puzzled look on her face. She turned the pages, confused. Re-read parts. Shook her head.

She began to cry again.

Ernst huffed with contempt. He walked out of the room, and stood in the hallway to listen.

After a moment, the crying slowed. "It is from the village where I was born, where I was a little girl. It is from Oma, my mother, and she says that things are very good there. The fields are full and there are bunnies, and a cow, and Opa is doing good, but he is getting old. And the village has grown, and there are new baby goats. Have you seen baby goats in the square? You have? Opa and Oma have several and they are so cute. Do you like baby goats? We shall see them someday. Someday we will see Opa and Oma, and see their goats and my village. Would you like that?" There was a pause. "You would?! Oh, I would love to show it to you! Johann, you are so big now and you are almost big enough to travel."

The tiny silver bell rang from upstairs, which meant it was time to escort the general back to his carriage. As Ernst walked the general down the hallway, the general asked the same question he always asked.

"What is behind those doors?"

"Those are the refreshing baths, cold water, Sir."

"Ah yes, I remember now!" exclaimed the general.

Ernst smiled perfectly. "Of course, general."

"I'm not one for the cold baths. Took enough of those when I was in the army. I heard these Swedes like that sort of thing. I'm too old for a cold dunk, too old to start something new."

Ernst was not sure what to answer. So he smiled. "Sir."

"But if I were a young man, who wanted to start over, those might be just the ticket."

Christmas at the Schickelmans

John Deakins

1637

The misplaced Pequot/Englishman Eliezer St. Clair had homesteaded as a blacksmith on a creek short of West Point. The Dutch *patroon* Kiliaen van Rensselaer had given his family more than a dozen acres on the river's north side.

Gerhard Schickelman and his wife Anke Janssen had acquired trade goods and purchased a large block of hunting ground from the Tappan tribe, to become farmers at never-to-be Nyack. Minor European diseases had thinned the Tappans, and the Schickelmans had been

generous. There was no friction between the new settlers and their Indian neighbors. Three older Schickelman offspring and their families had farms inland, but the older couple built a farmhouse, dock, and barn on the Hudson's west bank. Crop-efficient European land-use gradually swallowed the land, despite good intentions. The Tappans wouldn't have understood land *ownership*. As far as they were concerned, they'd agreed not to hunt and fish in that territory, nothing more. They paid little attention to the Schickelmans.

Almost by accident, the Dutch couple had become friends of the St. Clairs and their adorable daughter. Anke, her children gone from home, had heart-space for more grandchildren and a yen for match-making. The half-English/half-Oneida toddler would grow into a beautiful woman, at just the right age to be courted by a Schickelman grandson. The St. Clairs also had two younger sons who might someday fancy a Schickelman granddaughter. Her opportunity came when the St. Clairs adopted a pair of native teenagers, Green Star Passes and Willow Branch.

The blacksmith's family regularly passed the Schickelman farm, a good resting place when traveling with women and children. Young and inexperienced, Green Star never stood a chance. Arrow (his adopted mother), Anke Janssen, and Clara van Tanken, their New Amsterdam friend, had determined that Willow Branch was his logical mate. Willow Branch liked the idea. They all leaned on him. Eventually, the couple became *Caughnawagas*, "Christian Indians." They were married in the New Amsterdam Calvinist church. The three conniving women were ecstatic. Though stay-at-home Gerhard Schickelman had been reluctant, he'd been dragged to the "town" ceremony, anyway.

Upset by events along the coast, Eliezer decided that the time had come to move on. He, Arrow, their two infant sons, and their beloved daughter, Thunder, departed for the Iroquois country in the spring of 1637. The only good news was that Green Star and Willow Branch had produced another adorable daughter for Anke to spoil. Little Nieuwjaar (New Year) St. Clair would turn one year old as 1638 arrived. That was more important than any French invasion of Massachusetts.

* * *

"Gert, it's time we had a real Christmas celebration." Anke Schickelman dried her hands on her skirt. "We're here. We aren't leaving. The house and barn are built. The crops are in. The livestock are fat. Things have been tight in past years, but that's not true now." Her lined face was alive with anticipation.

Gerhard Schickelman looked up from some minor project. "Certainly, Anna. The children and grandchildren will be here. We—" She snorted in derision. She walked over and stood over his gray head.

"Gerhard Schickelman, you'll prove to all and sundry that Dutchmen are cheapskates! I mean a *real* celebration, a feast with friends, as we did in the old country."

"Just who were you planning to invite?" This early in November, he might be able to talk her out of it.

"The St. Clairs, of course," she said.

"You don't fool me, Anke Janssen. This will just be an excuse to celebrate little Nieuwjaar's first birthday." He frowned and combed his fingers through his winter beard. "They'll want to bring that scarred Indian that stays with them. Returned. He's so odd."

"Who'll he have to bring him Christmas joy, Gert, if not us?"

He grunted, but struggling would be a waste of time. "Of course..."

She smiled distantly.

"Of course, what? Who else are you planning for us to feed?"

"I want to invite my friend Clara van Tanken and her family. I got on well with her when we went to town for the wedding. They gave us a place to sleep, after all. You spent plenty of time with Simon and the boys."

He was still determined to sulk.

"'Spent time?'" she said. "The lot of you flopped down in the lumberyard, drinking Clara's good beer and smoking your pipes. You spent hours out there, listening to Eliezer tell tall tales about that wonder city from the future."

The truth mildly embarrassed him.

"Anke, they have family in New Amsterdam. Won't they want to stay there?"

"Simon has no kin on this side of the ocean, and Clara's cousins aren't on speaking terms with them right now, because of politics. It'll be a lonely Christmas for that family, unless we bring them here." She noted his reluctance. "If Clara can't share her good beer with her cousins, she's bound to bring some." That cast an entirely new light on the gathering as far as Gerhard was concerned. Anke spotted the moment to spring the remaining list on him.

"I also want to invite Heinrich Brinkerman, the governor-general's former clerk, and his wife. Some in town won't talk to them because he was too good to the St. Clairs. He was dismissed from his job. They have few friends, and they're good people. She's a shy thing. I met her at the wedding." She hurried right on, adding the next invitation before Gerhard could object. "I want to invite Pastor Bogardus. Think about having a man of God offer the prayer over our Christmas feast. Some don't like him because he's not radical enough, though he's a good Calvinist. He's always behaved like a Christian toward all the St. Clairs."

Gerhard Schickelman groused and muttered, but it was a fight that he couldn't win.

"Wait," he said. "What about *Pakjesavond* on December 5th? How many presents will we be giving then? That's too many for all to have presents. You'll beggar me."

"Call it what you will. We'll have the family here for the *Sinderklaasvond* on the 5th. That's early in December after all. The Van Tankens will probably celebrate it with their boys, anyway. The St. Clairs are new to our ways. We'd best give them the extra time. The Brinkermans and Pastor Bogardus will be surprised and need more time. Before *Eerste Kerstdag* on the 25th, the river should be frozen like a stone. Travel will be cold, but easy.

"We'll give our children and grandchildren their presents from us on St. Nikolas' Day. The young ones are too small to appreciate *Sinder Klaas,* but your older children (Do they ever grow up?) will expect a riddle from you in their wooden shoes, on where you've hidden their present. You old rascal!" She hugged him, itchy beard and all, and he smiled. His arms didn't reach as far around her as they once did, but they were warm, as was she.

"Wait," he said. "What about the 'surprise' gifts? We usually give them on *Sinderklaasvond*, too."

"This year, it will be a 'surprise' gift for the whole company. We'll have presents on the 25th, *Eerste Kerstdag*, and continue the feast on *Tweede Kerstdag*, the 26th. There should be eighteen persons old enough make and to receive a 'surprise.'"

"How is that supposed to work? It's plain that you planned all this without consulting your husband. What if I'd said, 'No.'?"

"And would that have done you any good?" she asked. He mumbled to himself, but a question still remained. She continued, "I'll write each name on a bit of paper, with more information, and sew it into a scrap of old cloth. Watch. Green Star will come down the river ice and stop here to get warm. He carries those spiked horseshoes to New Amsterdam several times a winter. That's his family's living. We'll give him the 'surprise' names for his family, the Van Tankens, the Brinkermans, and Pastor Bogardus. He can carry them into town."

* * *

By late November, the river was fully frozen. Green Star, towing a loaded sled, stopped at the Schickelmans'. He understood feasting and the yuletide gathering. Mohawks often feasted after the winter solstice. Everyone felt happy when the sun turned north again. His father had mentioned that some Dutch had special get-togethers then. He brought other news.

"We have two more guests in our longhouse: Clear Water, a Mohican girl of twelve, and Spider, her brother. He's seven. We must bring them." He omitted baby Daisy, because she was too small to understand gifts. Anke Schickelman was flustered because her count was then off, but she recovered quickly.

"Remain here until I prepare two more 'surprise' names and messages." Frau Schickelman had the same unstoppable inevitability that his mother, Arrow, had had.

He waited. Secret messages in hand, he agreed to make deliveries and to bring his extended family on December 24th. They ascertained the current date, November 22nd. It was easy to lose track of calendars in the New Netherlands wilderness.

The Van Tankens in New Amsterdam were always glad to see him. The invitations delighted them. Pastor Bogardus was gracious, because Everard was always gracious. He'd be glad to be out of town for Christmas. Hot-heads were still talking upheaval. That ruined an otherwise peaceful season.

* * *

Green Star returned to St. Clair Forge mildly puzzled. Horseshoe sales had gone well, with seasonal prices high. Traffic on the frozen Hudson was reaching winter maximum. That wore out horseshoes. The feuding sides had declared unofficial truce for the Christmas season and the winter weather. Still, he'd barely heard of Christmas himself, and he'd definitely never heard of surprise gifts. He explained it as best possible to his expanded family. The celebration was new to them, but they understood feasts and gifts. Then, he handed each the name of their "surprise" person.

"There'll be too many people for us to give every person a gift, but each will concentrate on the single person in your message. Willow Branch and I can read Dutch, to keep our 'surprise' name a secret. We'll read the names for Returned, Clear Water, and Spider. Each will try to keep our gift as much a secret as we can. We'll help one another, but we won't notice more of the secret than we can help." The youngsters were delighted.

"I am included?" Returned was confused. He looked up at Green Star with a face that would never again be quite normal, even for a former Mohawk.

"You've met Herr Schickelman. He knows you're coming. You're New Year's 'uncle,' after all."

"Is this some special 'spirit' ceremony?" Returned asked. As far as he was concerned, life at St. Clair Forge existed on the border of some spirit world.

"In a way. Some of the Dutch see it as a celebration of Jesus' birth. Mostly, though, it's a celebration of family, friends, feasting, and gift-giving."

The damaged native cast his eyes downward and asked no more. His inclusion spawned feelings he hadn't experienced in a long time.

"What about baby New Year and baby Daisy?" Willow Branch asked. "No secret names for them?"

He snorted, showing his doubt. "Frau Schickelman counts New Year as her granddaughter. You know that she'll feed all her grandchildren until they pop, and there'll be a gift for each. In a few years, New Year will be able to draw a name, but not now.

"While I'm thinking about it, we need to speak Dutch only, until the feast arrives. I speak it often, but I still need practice. Willow Branch, you speak it sometimes when you visit Clara Van Tanken or the Schickelmans, but you need even more practice. Returned, you speak it about as well as Willow Branch, but you haven't spoken it in months. We must teach Clear

Water and Spider all we can. There'll be a dozen people there that speak Dutch only. We must be ready, or we'll seem like simpletons. Let's begin.

"Oh, when I delivered the invitation to the Brinkermans, Frau Brinkerman came to the door. She called for her husband right away, and then scurried off like a chipmunk. I almost laughed, but that would have been rude, after Herr Brinkerman was so helpful to us. I was dressed mostly like a Dutchman, but she acted as if I was about to scalp her." He chuckled. "The Mohawks did invent scalping."

* * *

Clas van Tanken was hostile, as only a thirteen-year-old can be hostile. "I have the name of some twelve-year-old *girl*. How could I know what to get her?"

Clara, his mother scowled and seized his ear. "You aren't supposed to be braying the name of your secret surprise person. You're so proud of becoming a man soon. You were twelve yourself a year-and-a-half ago. Think about what things you wanted then."

Across the room, his father, Simon, offered no ear-relief. "I'm considering sending you to apprentice as a blacksmith with Green Star next year. Don't make an enemy of some girl living in his house. Close that mouth, and start using your imagination."

* * *

"Heinrich, send a message by that Indian man to Anke Schickelman," Kaatje Brinkerman called to her husband. "I'll make the ring-cakes for the whole gathering this year. It's the least I can do. I have those spices that that English ship brought up from the Indies. They will make the ring-cakes special, and I know Frau Schickelman will be very busy."

"That should be no problem, Kaatje," he replied, on his way into the white New Amsterdam weather. "I'll leave a message at Thyssen's stable. He's one of Green Star's best customers." Being reminded of the

Schickelmans' celebration nudged the pain he felt. There'd be only two Brinkermans attending. Both wanted children, but their marriage had been barren.

* * *

Thus it was that the companies journeyed to mythical Nyack. Heinrich Brinkerman and Kaatje rented a horse-and-sleigh, though Kaatje was wide-eyed at the cost. On Christmas Eve morning, they picked up Pastor Bogardus. The six-mijlen drive was beautiful, with the glistening snow on every side and the ribbon of the Hudson stretching before them. The men's presents took up little space, but Heinrich couldn't discover Kaatje's present at all. Perhaps she'd hidden it under the ring-cakes.

The Van Tankens' wrapped presents didn't mass much, but the beer-keg, upon which Clara had insisted, weighed down the toboggan. Though she was pleasingly plump and though it was a long walk to Nyack, Clara took turns towing the sled. It was a "Christmas" thing to do. On the clear center ice, the boys circled the sled on their hardwood skates, shouting. By the time the four had reached the Schickelmans', the boys were doing no more than keeping up.

The St. Clairs left West Point hours before dawn on the 23rd and arrived in the darkness. Willow Branch, her pregnancy showing, rode wrapped up, with the two babies bundled close to her.

"Anke Schickelman will be astonished that we suddenly have two children!" Willow Star laughed. The smaller 'surprise' presents rode with her, as Returned and Clear Water towed her sled. Green Star had been adamant that she'd be doing no pulling. He had his own sled, loaded with his covered gift, Spider's gift (hidden in a piece of deerskin) and a gutted, skinned deer carcass. Spider insisted on sharing the load with his mentor.

After thirty kilometers, they took a break for food and hot tea. Everyone needed to stretch and walk about, extending cramped muscles and seeking isolated brush for other purposes. They warmed at a fire in the shelter of some evergreens. The moss under the babies needed changing, they were hungry, and they didn't appreciate snow used to clean their bottom. The second half of the journey was hard work before the Schickelmans' sturdy dock appeared. The lead sled-pullers were dragging their feet, and Spider had decided to "help" Green Star by riding with the deer. The sky was clear and starry, but the land had been almost empty. They insisted on sleeping in the barn's hay. They'd officially "arrive" the next day.

With each new arrival, Gerhard was at the door, calling, "*Vrolijk Kerstfeest!*" Anke was cooking, but she greeted every guest with joy.

"Kaatje! It's so good to see you! Put those ring-cakes over there. I'm sure they'll be wonderful." (Frau Brinkerman blushed as she complied.) Clara, *welkom*! Such handsome sons you have! Willow Branch, what is this? Another baby? Have you—? No, I see that you haven't. You must tell me all about it. And who are these beautiful young people with you?"

"This is baby Daisy." Willow Branch let Anke see the Mohican baby's face by lifting the flap at the carrier's top. "This is my sister-of-the-spirit, Clear Water, and this is— Where did he go? For that matter, where are all the men?"

"We have prepared the barn floor for the feast." Anke brushed flour from her hands. "We can't be burning down the barn just to warm it for a meal. Gerhard and the boys have been raking the floor and building stone circles for yuletide fires, but I suspect that he's now checking to see whether Clara's good beer has survived from New Amsterdam. The lot of them need to figure out how to cook that deer tomorrow for the *Tweede Kerstdag* feast. Our grandchildren will be here as soon tomorrow as the children can walk from their homesteads."

* * *

Everyone was tired. Brinkerman had put their horse away in a back stall, rubbing down its sweaty flanks. After a while, no one noticed the barn-smell anymore. Both house and barn followed the same pattern. Each was two stories, but each second floor was only a half-floor. In the old country, a family sometimes lived on the second floor, over the barn. A Dutch barn was cleaner than many houses. With timber plentiful in the New World, the older Schickelmans had built separate structures, mostly of logs. They'd gone up quickly at the hands of a healthy farmer, with two grown sons and a son-in-law to share the work. The barn's upper half-story was for hay, and the bottom for animals. Gerhard had had his grown children move the farm dogs, the oxen, and milk cow to their cabins, to free up the barn space for the feasts.

Their home's roof was supported by a single, central, glass-hard white-pine post, with two ridge poles forming a "T" left and right. Both upper ends had doors that could ventilate the half-floor in hot weather. With the doors closed, heat from the house's single fireplace would keep sleepers warm. The warmest place in the house was the floor in front of the fireplace, though the second floor always offered better sleeping. Anke noticed Willow Branch eyeing the ladder to the second floor apprehensively. At her stage of pregnancy, ladders weren't her friends.

"Willow Branch, my friend, you and your husband will sleep on a pallet in that corner, with your babies close at hand. Are they weaned? Best take care of that soon. In a few months, there will be a new St. Clair who wants their place. Oh, to be young again, when the blood runs hot! You will find it quite a load to have one nursing and two still toddling about, getting into things. I did myself. Walter and Rinus are only twelve months apart. I let them get to be three and four before I had Tryne." She sighed, remembering.

"They can eat solid foods, but I have been nursing them on this trip, for convenience," Willow Branch said. "They are hungry all the time. Do you have—?" She'd been unloading the infants from their carriers. They were sitting on the puncheon floor, entranced by the new sights and smells around them.

"I have some corn mush from breakfast," Anke said. "It will be warm in the fireplace soon. We'll add some honey. What little angels! In a dozen years, they'll be breaking my grandsons' heart." One of the "little angels" was crawling toward the fireplace. Anke reached out and snagged a handful of baby clothes. "We'll make them a pen in your corner, once they're fed, and they should be happy watching all the bustle until bedtime. Kaatje, Clara, you've had time to rest, and the St. Clairs are tired, too. They've had twice as far to travel. Come help with the babies." Though she didn't stop talking, she'd also never stopped cooking. By the fireplace light, she'd be up hours yet, tending the pots on the fire and in the attached oven.

With warm mush and honey, and a warm lap on which to sit, the babies didn't resist the wooden spoons feeding them. Kaatje was silent as she fed Daisy, but Kaatje was usually silent. Only her eyes showed her delight and sadness. After being fed, the pair were cleaned up and boxed into the corner, wrapped in blankets. The fed infants were soon asleep. They were used to noise in an even smaller space.

* * *

The outhouse behind the house was busy before bedtime, enough used it to keep the frost off the seat. No one wanted to be the first for another cold 'surprise' in the morning, but somebody had to be. The three boys, to no one's amazement, chose to sleep in the barn's hayloft. Giggling like girls, they raced up and down the ladder, but the first time Spider snuggled into the hay in his blanket after sundown, he was out of it. Despite their intention to play, the Van Tanken boys soon followed.

All the adults were warm. The house's upper floor, with leftover cooking heat, was excellent. Green Star and Willow Branch curled up near the babies' pen. Gerhard finally pressured Anke to let the fire die down and join him on a pallet on the floor. Only Clear Water was doubtful, but she finally wrapped in a blanket near the Iroquois couple. That was easier than rough travel had been with her parents.

* * *

Gerhard and his "boys" had spent days cutting extra wood. In the barn, trestle tables were set on tall blocks from the same trees. The four barn corners held four stone circles for deadwood fires. The sleepy boys in the loft wouldn't appreciate the loft windows being partly open, but the fires were smoky at first, and ventilation was necessary. The smoke brought them down to the morning fires. After a trip to the "man" place behind the barn, they raced to the house, hunting breakfast. Anke had a huge kettle of oatmeal ready, with honey and butter to improve it. She let each boy toast a large bacon strip on a green branch before she chased them away from her fireplace.

Everyone stirred, rearranged clothing, and did morning things. Oatmeal was good, but the real feast would be later in the day. Hungry babies got oatmeal, thinned with plenty of butter. Kaatje and Clara would let no one else handle the feeding. Frau Brinkerman gloried in holding any child, and Clara had once lost a daughter to smallpox.

It was easy to overlook Pastor Bogardus. He greeted everyone warmly, but he retreated to a corner and simply drank in the love swirling through the great log house's air.

Grown people pretended that food was the thing for which they were waiting, not some surprise *Kerstdag* gift. Youngsters would be scolded if they whined to open presents early. The Schickelmans' extended family arrived two hours after daylight, almost together. Walter and Rinus looked like twins, with wispy beards and hearty Dutch faces glowing with the cold. Their wives, the Botterman sisters, were stair-stepped in age, with Wilma two years older than Dael. Both were warm, round, and happy, each carrying a wrapped infant. Daniel Egmont stayed close to his pregnant wife, Tryne Schickelman, carrying his toddler son and pulling a sled loaded with gifts and covered pots. All lived only a couple of miles away. The four farms would someday expand to become a community's core. Perhaps they'd resurrect the name Nyack. Who knew?

The cries of *Prettige Kerst!* and *Zalig Kerstfeest!* rang inside and outside the house. The four young people found themselves underfoot, with no particular desire to be introduced to any more adults. Worse, if they fell under Anke's eye, she'd put them to work. They retreated to the second story and sat, looking down on the crowd. Clear Water ended up sitting next to Clas van Tanken. He almost retreated, but something radiated from her that he's never detected from any girl before.

After the meet-and-greet, the necessary unwrapping of infants, the insertion of Wilma's large turkey into Anke's oven, the attachment of Dael's heavy ham to a fireplace spit, and the moving of Tryne's pots to warm near the fire, the crowded company gathered around the walls. From the beginning, this had been Anke's celebration. She moved to the floor's central space.

"We've decided not to give presents this year," she said. She moved to return to cooking. There were indignant mutters. Those would have been followed by anger...until they saw her ruddy face bursting with laughter.

"Mother," Tyne called, "we'll get you for this! Who's first?"

"Jehu van Tanken. Come down." He'd scampered down the ladder before shyness struck him. She beckoned. "Stand here. Who is your present for?" He squirmed, but the happy group was having none of it.

"Daniel Egmont. It's in the loft. Clas, throw it down to me. It won't break." Daniel came forward and tore open the crude paper wrapping. "It's a hammer," Jehu said. "Every man needs a hammer. I made a little furnace, and I made an iron bloom from some ore. Green Star forged out the head, but I cut and polished the handle for you from applewood." With Daniel's delighted thanks, Jehu headed for the ladder again.

"Not so fast," Anke called. "You now get to sit by the fireplace and turn the spit so that the ham doesn't burn. That's why you were first. The man Returned is next." The damaged Mohawk took Jehu's place, but he looked desperately at Green Star.

"Rinus Schickelman," Green Star said. Returned gestured at the younger head of his family. Green Star continued, "Come forward, but wait." Returned hurried out to the barn and came back with an all-wood crossbow and a bundle of arrows.

The older Mohawk said, "I cannot do the spirit-magic with iron like Green Star, but this is for ducks and pigeons. The arrows are what the *Tehawrogah* use for ducks on the water." Rinus thanked him, but neither knew what more to say.

"Willow Branch," Anke called.

She rose with difficulty and came forward. "Kaatje Brinkerman will receive my present." The clerk's wife blushed but came forward, carrying Daisy, to receive a deerskin purse, decorated with beads and dyed quills.

"It's lovely," the clerk's wife said. Without thinking, she gave Willow Branch a hug. Both blushed then. Kaatje really couldn't interact with other people without that.

"Walter," Anke called her oldest son to the center.

The tall Dutchman called Dael Botterman's name. "I have a fine blanket for my sister-in-law. A trapper on his way to trade with the Tappan exchanged with me for a night's rest and an elk hide and its leg bones."

"I will give mine next to Green Star," Anke said. She handed the blacksmith a homespun shirt. "You are as big as my sons now, but you ruin all your shirts with sparks. Wear this when you go to town or come here next year for the feasts." He shook it out and noticed the green silk star sewn on the left breast. He thanked Anke and hurried to show Willow Branch and his family.

"Clara," Anke called next.

The round lumberman's wife grinned as she gave Gerhard a brass beer-mug with a letter "G" engraved on the side. "An English sailor named Samuel traded it to me for a gallon of beer and a wooden cup. I never met a man who appreciates my beer like you do." He laughed and agreed.

"If the rascal's name was Samuel, he probably stole this mug somewhere!" Herr Schickelman commented.

"Gert, just stay there and do your gift," Anke said, frowning at him.

"Very well. My gift is for the man Returned." From his vest, he produced a clay pipe. "When the men sit and smoke, you can join us. I found a small deposit of pipe-clay, and I saved enough for a pipe. I cooked it in the back of the fireplace and made the stem from maple." Returned held it reverently. He looked up to say that it was too fine a gift, but Gerhard's face stopped him. He bowed his head and retreated.

"Rinus," his mother called.

"I have the name of Willow Branch. For her, a buffalo robe, to keep her and her children warm. That same trapper got a hog front-quarter from me. There were a few holes in the robe, but Dael fixed them for me." Willow Branch was joyous. The buffalo were seldom seen so far north as the Hudson, but she had heard of their valuable hides.

Anke brought the Dutch minister to center next. "Pastor Bogardus, ready?" The Calvinist pastor was usually a man of many words.

"I have young Jehu's name. Spider, come and take his place turning the spit." Green Star translated into the Mohawk tongue that Spider understood better. "Jehu, when I preach, I pay attention to who is listening. You always pay attention. Perhaps you will be a minister someday. Here is my prayer book, from when I was your age. Keep it well." The happy boy thanked him.

"Green Star," Anke said.

"I have Walter's name. I must go outside to fetch your gift. Clas, I will need Spider. Please take his place." Clas was reluctant to move, though he didn't understand why. As a dutiful youngster, he complied, but the teenager frowned all the way down the ladder.

Green Star was straining as he worked his gift through the door. "I'm a blacksmith, after all. It's a steel turning plow, like my father taught me to make. The fittings are wrought iron, but I didn't do a great job on the handles. They're beech-wood, because I found a couple of limbs shaped right. You may need to shape them better for your hands."

Walter couldn't have been any more excited. "Shaping will be the least of my worries. I wish you'd also brought me a club." Green Star looked puzzled. "I will have to fight my brother, my brother-in-law and my father to keep them away from my plow!" That brought on a general laugh. He carried the plow out the back door.

"Anke," Green Star said, "your gift from Spider is coming in now. He has kept it hidden from us for days. I don't know what it is." Spider did enter, dragging the biggest fish any of them had seen. It was still frozen, and it had been gutted. Spider needed both hands to keep the tail off the ground.

"I went ice-fishing while trying to think of a gift for you, and the Great Spirit sent me this fish. I kept it in the smoke-house, under a deerskin." Anke cradled it as she would a fireplace log.

"By the Moon and Sun, that kid is the luckiest fisherman I've ever seen!" Green Star muttered. "I've never caught a fish anywhere near that size."

"I— I— It's wonderful! I'll bake the whole thing, and you and I will share it at tomorrow's feast! Jehu, help him. Put it on the ledge outside a loft window to keep it frozen until I can get to it, and you shall share it with us two." Anke had just acquire two more grandsons. All exclaimed over the fish. The boys struggled up the ladder.

Wilma took their place in the center. She unwrapped a present about a meter long. "Clara, these are for you." She held a long-handled, two-pronged fork and an equally long set of wooden tongs. "No more burning your hands at the fireplace." (Wilma didn't know about the St. Clair stove that Clara used more than her fireplace.) The utensils would still come in handy.

"Wilma, just stay there. I have your gift," her sister-in-law Tryne said. "You're the writer among us. I traded a bushel of Daniel's maize for this." It was an inkwell, a steel-tipped pen, and a stack of good paper.

"Perfect!" Wilma called.

"Tryne, it's your time to stay in place," Simon said. He unwrapped a bolt of bright blue cloth. "As we visited in the lumber yard, your father bragged about your beautiful blue eyes. I traded some boards for this." Good commercial cloth was a rarity, and Tryne loved it. The simple "boards" had been some of Simon's finest finished lumber.

"Simon, I have your gift," Dael called. "I know that you're a pipe smoker. My father-in-law didn't use up all that good clay." Simon's new pipe was long-stemmed, almost the length of his forearm, befitting a proper Dutchman. He sat again, looking over his new toy.

"Who have we missed?" Anke said. Herr Brinkerman caught her eye. "Heinrich?"

"I have a gift for Spider. Long ago, my father got two of these, but my brother died of measles before he could receive his." Spider scrambled down the loft-ladder to receive a folding, wooden-handled knife. It was a man's knife, and he swelled accordingly. "Be careful. I still have scars on my hand from learning to use it."

Anke looked around.

"Daniel?" Anke had identified another gift-in-waiting.

"I made this for Pastor Bogardus," the Schickelman son-in-law said. "It's a crucifix carved from deer bones. The mounted colored stones are round New Amsterdam stones from a creek a few miles from here."

Everard Bogardus smiled. "It's a trifle on the Catholic side, but I'll still treasure it." The minister returned to his seat. Anke began looking about again.

"Clear Water, come down from there!" she called. "What do you have?"

"I have deerskin mittens for Clas van Tanken. The great hero, Manabozho, could knock mountains apart with his magical deerskin mittens." The ham on the spit was forgotten as Clas stepped up to try them on. "They will be warm, with the fur on the inside," she said. Perhaps he heard that, but his ears seemed to be roaring.

"I have your present as well," Clas stammered. "I have made you wooden skates like mine." Jehu pitched them to him from the loft.

"I—I don't know how to put them on or how to use them."

"I'll help you put them on and show you how to use them," Clas said. Who was that talking with my lips? Perhaps there were other persons in the great, warm room, but neither noticed.

Anke rolled her eyes to Heaven. Evidently God was a better matchmaker that she was. "For goodness sakes! Jehu come down and keep the ham turning. Who's left?" Silence settled for a moment.

"I am," Kaatje said. "I drew my own husband's name."

"Do you have a present wrapped for him?"

"No."

"No?"

"No. But I definitely have a surprise for him. Late in the summer, we should be having a baby." Silence reigned, then, pandemonium broke loose. Kaatje, who never raised her voice, raised her voice in triumph. "I have confirmed it with the lady physician in New Amsterdam, Anne Jefferson." Heinrich left his seat like a rocket and wrapped his arms around her. He didn't know whether to squeeze her in his delight or to handle her like porcelain. He spun her around and hugged her, as whispers explained their previously barren status. The whirl finally stopped.

He was all smiles. "No one has received as good a surprise as I did today! I was going to tell you all tomorrow, but I'll share my other news now. I've received a letter from Kiliaen van Rensselaer in Holland appointing me one of his factors in New Amsterdam. He distrusts the more radical Dutchmen here. I am gradually to dispose of his business holdings and his land, keeping ten percent for myself. Somehow, I impressed him as an honest man. When he heard that Van Twiller had dismissed me, he wrote. Green Star, as I sell his land, I'll see to it that you receive the best neighbors at St. Clair Forge.

"Anke Janssen, it's the feast of *Eerste Kerstdag*. Let's feast now as the best friends ever! What do we do next?"

She was ready. "Men, carry the meal to the barn. Don't burn yourselves. Some of those pots are hot. Jehu, Spider, go with them and get those upper doors shut all the way. Put some dead wood on the fires. Kaatje, carry your ring-cakes, but come back. Clas and Clear Water—" She stopped to smirk. "Grab an ax from the woodpile and cut us a small evergreen: decent, but not too big for this room. It's already crowded. Clara, girls, go with the men and slice the trenchers. There are twenty who'll need one. I have a wooden spoon for each. Wilma, carry the spoons and knives." She put her fists on her hips. "Why are you standing around like somebody's lost sheep? Get moving!" They got moving.

* * *

Thus it was that the company of friends feasted. Only a rack remained of the turkey, which would go home to the dogs the younger couples had left tied up at home, and the ham bone would be the center of Anke's stew for the *Tweede Kerstdag* meal. Tomorrow would feature venison stew and more venison cooked on wooden skewers over the fire pits. Damaged trenchers went into the stew pot, though some feasters ate the heavy brown bread as part of their meal. Clay-coated potatoes, baked in the hot fireplace ashes, loaded with butter and salt, disappeared until only a few were left for the second feast. Every kind of vegetable abounded. None of Kaatje's ring-cakes saw the second day. Except for the babies, everyone drank beer.

Everard Bogardus delivered a memorable Christmas prayer over the food, but the odors were too powerful for him to be long-winded. He sliced the turkey. Babies were passed from hand to hand as the adults stuffed themselves. The smallest liked the corn/squash mush as well as grownups did. Ignoring the crusts, babies and toddlers liked the pumpkin pies' filling, too. There'd be no pies for the second day, either.

The winter sun set early, as it always did so close after the solstice. The women barely had time for a short visit in the house, mostly making over their three pregnant sisters. The men wanted to smoke their pipes and sit around the fires in the barn, but three had a wife and child to get home to a cold cabin. All would return tomorrow for a proper get-together. Stuffed with good food and a bit beer-headed, the rest bedded down early. Both Clas and Clear Water had trouble sleeping, but they welcomed the dreams that arrived. Babies slept as babies sleep, not always conveniently for the adults who watched them.

* * *

Christmas' second day would involve less feasting and more visiting. The three satellite families arrived at mid-morning. After a bowl of Anke's stew, which had been simmering all night, the men adjourned to the barn to toast venison, smoke their pipes, and tell exaggerated stories. They sent a huge platter of venison slices inside, to be cooked over the fireplace coals and took along large loaves of brown bread to go with their own deer meat. Thoughtlessly, they hadn't planned to leave any beer for their mates. The women substituted talk about things that women won't talk about with men present, as they decorated the evergreen with the few apples that Anke had managed to preserve until December.

Early in the afternoon, almost everyone returned to the house. The tree was hung, not just with apples, but with *banketletters*. The letter-cookies had each been baked into some guest's first initial. Some of the women vowed to hard-bake theirs and put them away in remembrance of the first Schickelman feast. Men, who preferred cookies to remembrances, ate theirs, as did the boys. Babies teethed on hard, non-letter cookies.

In a corner, Spider whispered, "Where are your brother and my sister? And where are your boots?" Jehu looked disgusted.

"Your sister had no boots. There was no way to fasten on her skates. Clas threatened to beat me up later unless I loaned her mine. I have her moccasins. They fit pretty well, I guess. If you wanted to see something *stupid*, you should have watched him as he put the boots and skates on her. He couldn't keep his eyes off her legs, and he took *forever*. They're out on the river skating together. I'll bet he's *holding her hand* in his new mittens, to *help* her. Girls are so stupid. My brother has gone stupid, too."

"Yeah. Do you want to play outside?" Spider asked.

"Yeah. Sure! We'll build a snowman."

"I don't know how to do that."

"It's easy. I'll show you. C'mon!"

Only darkness ended the good fellowship. The women hugged Wilma, Dael, and Tryne as they headed for their cabins. The men shook hands and slapped one another on the shoulder. Everyone vowed to repeat the gathering next year, but they knew that even the future's best wouldn't equal the first loving feast. The fireplace fire was banked, and the camp-fires in the barn were allowed to die down, but not before thawing the half-frozen youngsters. The winter stars twinkled brightly in the night sky as those who remained headed toward exhausted sleep.

* * *

The dawn brought separation. New Amsterdam was still six mijlen downriver. St. Clair Forge upriver would require a long break and an arrival under really late winter stars. Two young hearts weren't exactly broken, but they were bruised, healing only when the next summer arrived.

Despite the hardships, the yuletide glow would last through white cold until the green came again.

No Proper Carol

Sarah Hays

November 29, 1638

"Mama," Marty Haag Ballantine said. "Have you ever heard the song about the herd of haunted cattle?"

Alyse Ballantine, surprised at the breakfast table, asked, " 'Ghost Riders in the Sky'?"

He nodded.

"Sure," Alyse said. "I like Roy Clark's instrumental best, but my favorite singer for that song is Marty Robbins. Why?"

"Because," he replied, "That song would make a great solo piece for band contest."

Alyse chuckled. "I think you're right. Were you thinking of guitar or recorder for playing it?"

"Fiddle," he replied firmly. "Well, I guess it would be violin. But no other student would have that piece, for that instrument, for a contest solo."

"*Sin duda, hijo,*" she said, and grinned again as his eyes lit up. Young Martin Haag Junior, since he'd come to live under Alyse's roof, had grown quite a lot; among the things he'd learned his way around, clearly, Spanish from Alyse's South Texas background could be numbered. The Haags first caught the Glazer family's attention when Powell befriended Martin Senior at church. Martin Haag had a beguiling baritone singing voice so close to bass he usually sang that part in the choir; his wife could be found in the church kitchen before almost any service where children would be present setting out treats for the youngsters. Alyse's penchant for making the kind of coffee the church's male members liked put the two in contact often.

When Martin's wife died from an illness Grantville no longer possessed the up-time drugs to stop, Powell found a sawmill job for former teamster Martin Senior so the widowed singer could be home every evening to care for his children. A few months later Powell took a job in Bamberg. Things percolated along for the two families fairly normally, until an accident in the sawmill cost Martin both legs. His wounds turned septic, and when he passed away, Powell and Alyse fostered his children with the intent to adopt them.

Martin Junior, shortly after moving in, figured out that he adored music from the up-time. He liked what the up-timers called classical music, and enjoyed religious music, too; he enjoyed show tunes and jazz, but his passion blazed up in particular heat for ballads. A performance during the Fourth of July festivities when the Old Folks Band took the stage left him thoroughly smitten.

The Voice of America reinforced his liking for what presenters called country and western music, but Martin found out about "cowboy songs," listening to a special program one Sunday night. He'd already been enchanted by the sounds of The Sons of the Pioneers first, then by Michael

Martin Murphey, Chris LeDoux, and Marty Robbins. Shortly after discovering the latter, Martin Junior started insisting on being called Marty. He listened, for hours on end, to Alyse's records, copied at the Trommler studio from her compact discs.

Alyse had watched all school year as the boy's growth changed him. Unlike Taylor, Marty remained wiry, his build inherited from his mother. Like his dad, Marty had dark hair with a distinct tendency to curl, and shining brown eyes he often closed in delight as he played guitar or listened to music. Then he grew out of the last of his Thuringian wardrobe just as Taylor outgrew last year's school clothes. Marty adopted the hand-me-downs with real alacrity, persuading his sister Jakobina to embellish a few pieces he wore while playing. If he'd lived up-time, Alyse thought, his walls would sport posters of classic country singers in Nudie suits.

"I have a problem, though," Marty said. Alyse raised her brows. Her clutch of children paused in their pursuit of breakfast, which consisted of biscuits stuffed with butter and preserves, or slices of bacon-and-cheese omelets. The boy set his biscuit on his plate and took a swallow of milk before explaining. "I can't find a usable version of the score for the song."

Not herself a musician, Alyse understood the difficulty anyway. He could no more practice properly without sheet music than one of her courier students could learn the Pony Express mail exchange without having saddlebags.

"*Hay un problema gravamente,*" she agreed, and took a judicious sip of coffee. "Does your band instructor have the music you need?"

Taylor Glazer shook his head while Marty took another bite. "No, Mom. I asked yesterday. That music wasn't part of anything either the junior high or high school bands had for marching or the sight-reading or concert contests. Mr. Wendell said he wasn't sure if a copy even came through the Ring, except in recorded performances."

"It must be in a songbook somewhere," Amanda Ballantine put in. Unlike her brother, she had adopted her mother's surname after their parents' divorce. She stopped long enough to finish chewing her bite of biscuit-and-preserves, washed it down with a swallow of milky coffee, and repeated herself in much more understandable terms.

"I looked at our school's library," Marty said sadly. "There is a 'guitar tab' version for Johnny Cash's arrangement. I don't know how to make the changes for violin in it. I haven't had a chance to go to the state library and ask yet."

Alyse smiled. "Let me check there for you, mi hijo."

He grinned, a drop of milk escaping to run down his chin. Though the state library accepted students' research requests, an adult's request might be answered faster. "Would you mind asking today?"

"Sure," she answered, forgetting for a moment that she couldn't just pick up the kitchen phone and call. The lack of a phone in the barn they'd moved into after the divorce remained one of her few regrets. Of course, the phone in the business office she shared with Pedro Sebastian Rafael de Treviño would do just as well. "How's your money for that fiddle coming along, by the way?"

"I can already afford a kit, and Mr. Bledsoe said if I buy it from him I can build it in his shop, and he'll even help me pick out the right finishes for the wood. I don't want..." he ran down, searching for a word. "It mustn't look too old."

The rumble of a motor in the driveway caught Alyse's attention. "That's up to you, but y'all are all about to miss the school bus."

Her four oldest children either gulped down morning drinks, shoved a final bite into cheeks that swelled chipmunk-fashion, or both. She watched them hustle to the door, each taking up a knapsack or a stack of books in a carrying strap on the way to catch the bus.

The screen slammed, and Alyse found herself surprised to hear Taylor calling back, "Mom!"

"Yes, *mi hijo*?"

"That piece of music is all Marty's talked about ever since the junior high band instructor asked him what he wanted to work up for spring contest," Taylor said. "I bet he'd love to get it for a Christmas present, this year."

She looked a question at him. "Are you volunteering to help?"

"I guess so," he said. "I mean, Marty nearly never asks for anything, Mom. He just works out how to get it by himself. I think he thinks this piece of music would prove to the Old Folks Band that he's good enough with their kind music to really impress the leaders. It' s his favorite of all the music to come through the Ring."

"I do," she said. "Thank you, Taylor, for letting me know."

He scuffed a shoe, pushed the screen aside, and headed out the door with alacrity. "Sure."

Alyse shut the door and turned back to gathering the older kids' dishes. She scraped the scarce leftovers into the scrap bucket to feed chickens later. Afterward she stacked dishes in the sink before she turned back to her two youngest. Mikey had eaten a biscuit and made inroads on his milk. Jessica Rose had just mopped the last of her omelet up on a biscuit-top of her own. Both would spend today at "Mother's Day Out," the drop-off daycare a few blocks from the office of the courier service Alyse and Pedro Sebastian ran.

Their courier service could stay in business because it went places air-mail couldn't, and other services wouldn't. Their biggest investor, H.A. Burston of Augsburg, insisted that they take packages too. Over the past year or so light cargo had come to dominate their workload. With Christmas less than a month away, they had a bit of a boom at the office, bringing an increase in income which gave Alyse money for a different "Mother's Day Out" Tuesdays and Thursdays. She liked doing so; it saved her driving all the way to Mountain Top twice daily. Her children liked it because they could play with friends.

She pulled the big saddle-colored Dodge onto the snow-dusted parking lot at First Baptist, today's host, with five minutes to spare. Jessica Rose squealed with delight at sight of her classmates, wriggling out of her booster seat without bothering to undo her seatbelt. She grabbed the door handle in both small fists, pushed it down with all her weight, and laughed as she jumped to the ground. Alyse called to her to wait, while she undid the child seat protecting Mikey.

"Mom," the little girl said, "It's Bambi day!"

"Okay, honey, okay," Alyse said, setting Mikey down, closing the truck door and reaching for her daughter's hand. Mother's Day Out at First Baptist had her daughter's favorite collection of movies, and Jessica Rose knew Bambi practically by heart.

A few minutes later she pulled into the parking lot beside the office. "Good morning, Pedro. Good morning, Angelina!"

Her partner smiled, waving the hand not holding his mug of coffee. Across the room, his wife looked up from her double-entry book-keeping, a skill learned from Luis Ybarra in the month they'd both had in the office. Angelina's new job as office manager had led, in Alyse's opinion, to a good many improvements in the atmosphere. She missed Luis, who had taken his dream job as "assistant apprentice engineer" at Leahy Medical with the prosthetics department. But Angelina brought a calm presence, as well as first-aid skills and a mending kit, to the workplace.

Luis still lived at Alyse's, paying her perhaps a third as much rent as a share of a room in Grantville cost. He walked the four miles to Leahy twice a day without complaint; her Christmas gift to him this year would be a particularly hard-headed big red roan gelding she'd gotten in partial payment from a Sundremda farmer. The farmer had finally given up trying to break the gelding from sighing hugely, falling to his knees between the traces of a cart or plow, and lying there until whoever harnessed him in gave up and unhitched him. The big horse otherwise obliged with great goodwill, not balking at carrying double or any amount of pack-weight.

The farmer had figured he'd make a good beast of burden for couriers. But the horse had too soft a mouth and gentle a temper for relegating to pack-work only. Luis rode as readily as he walked, and had made fast friends with the horse over the last half year, leading children around events as part of the business's outreach.

So, now, she had a perfect Christmas surprise for Luis, an unexpected present for Taylor in a pair of custom-made silver-chased spurs, a set of real steel crochet hooks complete with stitch markers and scissors shaped like a crane for Jakobina, a rainbow-ribbon-decorated skirt and straw sombrero for Amanda's *escamuerza* competition, the teddy bear Mikey had fallen in love with in the front window of Value Mart, and a set of Bambi sheets and pillowcase for Jessica Rose. She'd intended to pick up a set of guitar strings for Marty, but this piece of sheet music would be even better.

If she could find it.

Obvious sources would be either songbooks or recordings. One place that carried both for sale to the general public came to mind when she started leafing through Grantville's attenuated phone book. She called Trommler Records from the office phone, only to find out that not only didn't the company carry "Ghost Riders in the Sky" in its catalog, the clerk who answered the phone had never heard of the song. She thanked the man, hung up the phone, and said with a tired sigh, "I never thought I'd miss talking to Heather Mason, but there it is."

"There what is?" Pedro Sebastian asked.

Alyse poured a cup of coffee. "I miss talking to Heather Mason. She knew where to find about any song you could name."

"What song are you seeking?" Pedro Sebastian asked.

"It's an old song," Alyse said, "based on a cowboy legend. It's called 'Ghost Riders in the Sky.' When I was little, Roy Clark had a great big huge hit playing it on guitar. A few years later Johnny Cash put out a record of it that nearly went to number one on the country charts."

"I think I know that song," Angelina said. "Well. I have heard it, on the radio. It sounds like it's about the *Wilde Jagd*, to me."

Alyse gave her a puzzled look. Angelina explained the legend of the Wild Hunt. "Didn't you have anything like that?"

She thought that over. "No," she said finally. "We had UFOs." Explaining that took a while. Fortunately, four of their six students for the day did not appear for their lessons, and H.A. Burston telegraphed that a large shipment of goods expected in Grantville had turned up in Augsburg. He intended to send them onward using the steam-powered all-terrain vehicles based there.

"Alyse," Pedro Sebastian said, "why don't you take the rest of the afternoon and visit the library?"

She took him up on the offer.

The state library had become something of an obstacle course; Alyse spent nearly an hour in line to enter. When she finally reached a librarian, she learned that she needed to file a request for a particular songbook.

"I don't know," she said slowly, "which, if any, of these..." She gestured at the list of nearly fifty books the librarian offered with a sense of frustration. "...is the one I need. Can you help me narrow it down? Or can I look in the card catalog, for the song itself?"

The librarian smiled the kind of smile someone who has to say, "No," politely to about a hundred different versions of the same question every day, smiles. "I'm afraid not."

"Thanks anyhow." Alyse started to feel discouraged. Well, she had ten days before school let out, the day before Christmas Eve. She'd just have to figure out how to narrow down the candidate books by then. "Say, do any of these books contain actual sheet music?"

"No," the librarian said, but not as she had before. "If you want sheet music, there's another section to look in. We don't get nearly as many requests for that. I thought you wanted a book focused on music history."

"So did I," Alyse admitted. "But what I think I need is a simple copy of the score of the song."

"If you have a recorded performance, there's a group of students who might be able to help you with transcribing the score. Have a talk with Marcus Wendell, once band classes are over for the day."

Alyse nodded. "I'll call Marcantonio's Pizza and see if they've got it in their jukebox."

The young counter girl at Marcantonio's had no idea, clearly, what finding a song on a jukebox meant. She fetched her manager, who introduced himself a little grandly as Fabio and claimed he had worked in every pizza purveyor's place in town.

"We have the Johnny Cash record," he said. Alyse, who did not have the song on a record or a CD, listened to Johnny Cash's distinctive guitar backed by a tinny, bell-toned piano, and understood a good deal more about why Marty wanted a different arrangement of the song.

She thanked the manager and went to the band hall. The instructor had just finished with the day's last class when she arrived. "I'm sorry," he said. "I told Taylor I didn't have that score, and then I forgot all about it."

"I understand," she said. "Do you have any idea who might have a recording of it that isn't by Johnny Cash? I wore out the Highwaymen tape I had it on, before the Ring fell."

The band teacher shook his head. "I'll ask around, if you like."

"Please," she said. "And thank you."

Walking out she heard the bells at the middle school striking five and realized she'd probably be late at "Mother's Day Out." She cut a couple of corners on the way a little closer than she ordinarily would and arrived just as the line to pick up children cleared.

Wednesday went by in a blur of deliveries and riding lessons. Thursday she dropped the children off at the Methodist church, went in to work, and stared in dismay at the telephone message Angelina had taken from the state library. Five copies of the musical score were on file, all identical, all for the Johnny Cash version of "Ghost Riders in the Sky."

"It's the wrong song," she nearly snarled. "You'd think somebody'd have a copy of an old Hee Haw episode with Roy Clark playing it on guitar, at least."

"Hee Haw," Angelina said. "Isn't that what the Old Folks Band's music comes from?"

Alyse phoned the Thuringen Gardens. The Old Folks had played the previous Saturday and wouldn't play again until after New Year's. But the manager had a phone number for one of the women in the band.

Before she could call that number, a customer came in with a package that had gone to a wrong address, and then two of Alyse's students arrived to make up lessons missed earlier in the week. She remembered intending to call on her way to church to pick up the kids and snapped her fingers in disgust.

After daycare that evening, Mikey had bright red cheeks and a warm forehead, and Alyse forgot all about the quest for a copy of a song. Jessica Rose let herself be buckled in with uncharacteristic quiet. For the next solid week, Alyse found herself contending with two preschoolers miserably ill. Mikey threw up several times a day.

On the day before the last day of school before Christmas, Pedro Sebastian stopped in after lunch with a note. "The band director says he asked Mr. Buckner if they had the song. Mr. Buckner says he has an old VCR tape of Johnny Cash playing, but that's all. None of the Old Folks use sheet music, he said. They play by ear."

Alyse felt a spike of dread. Even if they'd found a recording, the group of students who did transcription already had orders enough to keep them busy through St. Valentine's Day.

"I guess that settles it," she said. Both her preschoolers had fallen asleep, deeply enough to mark recovery from illness; her other children would be home on the bus in an hour. "Pedro, if I give you the money, will you pick up a set of guitar strings for me? That way something'll be under the tree for Marty Christmas morning."

"Si," her partner said, suddenly serious. "Of course. I will get in touch with Mr. Bledsoe and find out which ones will be best for the guitar Marty has, yes? He teaches Marty, does he not?"

"He does," she said gratefully, and counted out twenty dollars.

"This is too much money." Pedro Sebastian was full of reproof.

"No," Alyse told him. "It's not. You are owed something for your trouble finding out which ones to buy, then buying them and bringing them back to me."

He made a growling sound, took the money, and left.

Alyse tried not to let on how her search for the sheet music had gone. She didn't quite catch what made Amanda and Taylor and even Jakobina act so upbeat. Alyse put it down to their school vacation starting in just one more day, if not Christmas two days after that.

* * *

On Christmas morning, the children woke before daylight. Alyse had been up late, not daring to start wrapping their surprises before she knew they'd gone to bed and fallen asleep. Under the tree, each child had at least four other packages—and by the way they'd been wrapped, the ones marked "From Mikey" and "From Jessica Rose" had had help from the older siblings. Someone even set aside a patterned paper bag with her name on the outside.

Instead of an ordinary breakfast, she put together pancakes laced with cinnamon and nutmeg, served with maple syrup. She calmly reserved the sausage and bacon in case last night's heavy snow kept up; Alyse wanted her household not to go hungry. She did make up some of her precious cache of cocoa, though, and took her own Christmas morning delight in watching the kids' faces as they tasted it.

Alyse spent half a chilly hour taking care of the horses in her pasture, catching up with Taylor and Amanda as they checked on the chickens and rabbits. Even Jessica Rose and Mikey should be ready to open presents, and perhaps Luis through with his coffee by the time they regained the house.

The prosthetics factory would not open today; it had closed at noon on Christmas Eve. Alyse hadn't let the children wake Luis, for he had come home from Christmas Eve Midnight Mass cold to the bone, wet to the knees, just as she finished the last of the presents.

Since the incident in Judge Tito's court where Luis slew the man who'd tried to kill him, the young man had grown far quieter, more dignified, almost driven in attending services. Alyse understood the change in him; she had felt similar urges when she first came home from Pomerania. But when she opened the front door, she heard laughter ringing from room to room: the kids had Luis home, and Luis had the kids to romp and play with on a day that wasn't Sunday, when he spent the morning at Mass.

"Mom," Taylor called as soon as he saw her. "Mom, come look. You have to see what Luis did!"

Amanda sat on a high stool between the fireplace and the home office, pedaling away on a strange-looking contraption. Behind her, gathered around Alyse's treasured 1990s "boom box," the rest of the kids were listening raptly to the radio's broadcast of Christmas carols. Jakobina leapt to her feet from a spot on the hearth and ran to Alyse, carrying a package.

"Luis brought us all presents–look, if we pedal this, we can have electricity in the house!"

She studied the thing for about three seconds and then smiled broadly. "That," she said, "is quite a gift, Luis."

"There's more, Mama." Jakobina pushed her packet into Alyse's hands. "Be careful with the paper–some of that's for Marty, you'll see when you open it. But what's inside, here, is for you. From all of us. Luis, too."

Alyse opened the brown outer paper delicately, turning it inside out as she went. On the inside, in a spidery hand, she found lyrics; a second sheet, this of a paper as supple as vellum, had been carefully folded to show a pair of musical staffs on the outside. On the inside, it carried four carefully-copied measures of music, each bearing a treble clef at its opening. She sank into a chair and held this out to Marty, who took it as delicately as though she had offered him a live hummingbird.

"I've never seen this kind of arrangement before," the youngster said softly.

"It's for vocals, and ukulele," Luis said. "I found it in a book about the first person who sang it professionally. His name was Stan Jones. That book was in the city library. They have a lot of what they call celebrity biographies there." He turned to look at Alyse. "One side of that tape is Chris LeDoux, on a record that came out of the jukebox the Club 250 used to have. The jukebox sold when the building converted, but I'm told it hadn't worked for years before that. The records seem not to have been damaged in the same way as the machinery of the jukebox."

"It says the second song," she noticed, "is The Borderline."

Luis nodded. "My friend Matti Antinpoika has a player like yours, and he's the one who bought this record at the auction. He bought about a dozen records, he told me. He had this song on two of them."

Alyse turned the cassette over. On the other side, the tape said simply, "Marty Robbins."

Tears welled up in her eyes.

"Curtis Maggard's boarder?" she asked Luis.

"Yep," Luis said, showing off an Americanism he'd picked up at the prosthetics factory. "Curtis taught him to be a bowyer and a hunter. But I believe he plans becoming a disc jockey. That's why he collects the records."

The rest of Christmas Day, everybody who could reach the pedals took turns at the generator to keep the radio playing. In between, snacks and sandwiches and popcorn sustained everyone.

No one complained when the Christmas carols repeated over the Voice of America. Finally, as sunset outside folded into darkness sparkled by falling snow, the radio station announced the end of its broadcast day.

"All right, Marty," Alyse said. "Let's hear your song."

"It's not a Christmas carol, Mama."

"That's all right," Alyse said, pushing the pedals down for the beginning of her third, or maybe fourth, turn at the generator. "I think you should talk to Mr. Wendell, when you go back to school, about scoring your song for violin."

"Fiddle," the boy said firmly.

Alyse pedaled faster, and the CD player launched Chris LeDoux's voice into the evening. They listened to both sides of the tape, then Luis put the littler children to bed. Marty brought out his guitar, handed Jakobina his recorder, and they played together, puzzling out the handwritten score.

"Christmas carols," Taylor said with a wink at his mom, "don't impress contest judges much. It's a good thing you like this song."

As the fourth repetition began, Alyse had to grin. "It is."

Santa's Lapp

George Haberberger

North of the Ume River, Sweden
December, 1633

The sun came up in a different place than yesterday, Erik was sure. He was sitting on a pile of reindeer pelts, sitting so that a rock and a pine were aligned on his left, and two pine trees were aligned on his right. The same place he sat yesterday morning. He was also sure it had been coming up in different places for a few days; the days were getting longer. It was close to the time of the Grantville Christmas. He was ready.

Bracing himself with a walking stick, he pulled himself to his feet, groaning as his stiff leg didn't want to move. He gathered the pelts and an empty bottle and put them in a pack. It was going to be another sunny, clear, and cold day. He needed a sunny day, if the shaman agreed. The shaman might not, in which case Amund might wait another year. He slung the pack over his shoulder and went off to see Aikia.

Erik had to lay his cards on the table to get Aikia to agree to an early, daylight meeting. One more thing to be thankful to Grantville for, such a wonderful expression. It wouldn't have made sense to Aikia, but Aikia didn't spend weeks recovering from a broken leg desperate for something to pass the time. Card games were good for passing the time, and poker was a good card game. Erik was good at poker, and ended up spending some of his winnings on a prized deck of cards. He didn't bring much back from Grantville, but he brought back a deck of cards. Maybe he should teach Aikia poker. It was somewhat similar to card games they had played as children.

On the way to his tent, he asked his sister-son to wake him before the daylight meeting. All night meditations were wearying, and he didn't have any coffee left from Grantville. A few hours of sleep would help him. The sister-son's price was his retelling of seeing Loviatar in Grantville. He agreed; there was a good lesson there.

All too soon he was being awakened. At least the sister-son brought him a cup of soup. He could smell the acrid wood smoke; the fire had been started. After finishing the soup he went to the meeting, grimacing at the bright sunlight.

Aikia had gathered the tribe around the outdoor fire pit. "Erik has some tales of Grantville he must tell, and he needed the daylight to do it. There are Grantville artifacts you must see to understand his tale." Many of the younger people gasped. Grantville was known, Erik and a few others had even been there, but artifacts from there were rare. That made telling the tale in daylight sensible.

Erik walked in front of the tribe, close enough to the fire to feel some of the heat. "First, I will tell you again of seeing Loviatar. If I had not seen Loviatar I would not have a second tale to tell you." The children settled down.

"As you know, several of us traveled with the Swedes, we are good cavalry for them, and the money they gave us helped the tribe. Some of us will come back, some never will." Erik paused, mourning Ante. They grew up together, were best friends but one of Captain Gars' foes took his life in battle. It pained Erik that he forgot what battle it was.

"Captain Gars summoned us to ride to Grantville. The trackers had seen that many Croats were on their way to destroy the city. It was a long, hard, cold ride, and few Swedes could have done it. Our horses were weary and nearly spent when we arrived. We saw the Croats were attacking a large lodge, taller than a pine tree, longer than a reindeer herd. This lodge had openings high in the wall, and there I saw Loviatar. She was beautiful and powerful, wielding a thin musket with unbelievable accuracy. She knew Captain Gars, and Captain Gars was in her favor." The children up front stopped chattering, listening. They knew the story, and loved listening to Erik tell it.

"I was a bad warrior. I was too distracted by her unworldly beauty and power. That is the nature of gods, they are awe inspiring and make people forget themselves. Some Croats were too close to Captain Gars. Loviatar saw and removed one's heart with her gun. That Croat died, but his horse panicked and ran into my horse, and my horse panicked because I was still paying attention to Loviatar and not my tired horse. I survived the battle with a broken leg and other broken bones, and learned that even when a god approves of you, they are hazardous to be around. Their power can overwhelm mere mortals like us. Beware of them."

Erik took a break to refill his cup of soup and eat some dried berries and fish. He remembered falling onto the strange hot rock, and his horse falling on him. The battle ranged around him, hooves pounded near him, yet they did not step on his hands. Perhaps Loviatar favored him a bit, too.

The sun had started to dip. There wasn't a lot of daytime left. He sat down and continued.

"The people of Grantville are good and kind. After the battle they tended to the wounded. I woke up in a white bed softer than down, my wounds cleaned and covered, my ribs wrapped up and my leg splinted. They are not gods. They couldn't save Lars, and my broken leg will hurt until the end of my days. I spent a long time there. Captain Gars stopped to visit, even Julie, the woman who became Loviatar for a time." Erik paused for another sip, remembering how different Julie appeared at the foot of his bed. She seemed to be a normal, healthy pretty young woman, not a goddess of death.

"It was strange, and boring, to be confined in comfort all day long, have your wastes taken away and have food brought to you." Many laughed. Babies lived like that; everyone else worked every day. It would be nice to be bored like that.

"I noticed the healers would pick up a board and mark on it periodically. I asked what it was, they said they were recording my days. It wasn't just a tally of days, but how my wounds were healing, what healer had treated me, and even my name. They had ways of putting new thoughts, ideas and notices down on the board, for anyone to read." The tribe grew silent for a few moments. They remembered the Christian missionaries who read from their Bibles, but many hadn't realized that reading was more than tallying and reminders.

"Yes, it's odd and unsettling. Thoughts can be put down and read, even after a person has died. Lies can be put down and people may think they're truth. Legends can be changed. Did they even have people who remembered the legends and passed them down?"

"Those strange thoughts stayed with me for a long time. I left their healer's place, but still wasn't strong enough to ride with Captain Gars.

I worked for him in Grantville. Who knew knowing a little English and German would be so helpful. I translated for other men, I looked after horses, I helped the captain's newcomers to Grantville. Then, it struck me." Erik got up to walk around a little. In the cold his leg hurt worse when he was idle.

"If these Grantville people were from the future, and everything was written down to be read, even after the writer died, they might know what the future held for the Sami. I found out where they kept their written down knowledge. It was in the same building where I saw Loviatar." Erik paused and thought, much had happened at that school. Comrades had been hurt, some had been killed. Many Croats died, and he remembered being afraid of the many up-time devices. Then he went back to confront the future.

"I could not read, the up-timer children spent many winters learning to read and write, I couldn't do it in a few months. But I could hire people who could read and find out the future for me. I asked them to tell me what our homeland was like hundreds of years in the future."

"It was bitter fruit. Our homeland was divided between the Russ, the Swedes, the Norwegians, and the Finns. They were wolves, we were lemmings. We didn't have our own homeland. You Nils, you could not visit your grandmother Rika since she lived in land the Russ controlled, and you didn't. We weren't free to roam with our reindeer, old family ties were sundered. " Erik saw that there was not much daylight left. He had to finish.

"I spent more of my coin. A researcher found this treasure. It took much of my coin to get." Erik brought out a yellow bordered book with a stunning picture of a young Sami in front of a lodge. The colors leapt off the page, as vivid as life. Some of his people moved closer to look at it. The picture looked real. Erik showed that it was made of many thin leaves, and the leaves near the front held familiar pictures of their lives. He handed it to Aikia, who passed it along.

"The up-timers made this magazine in untold numbers, and every month a new one arrived. This one is about us, in the up-time. The researcher read it to me. We were a nearly forgotten, rustic, dwindling people. Our future was bitter, indeed."

Erik paused for more soup. The sunlight was waning, becoming golden and mixed with red from the fire. "I was despondent, not wanting to return here and bring bad tidings. So I felt until we neared their Christian God's birth celebration."

Some of the people hissed, others made warding signs. Christians were not loved among their people. Many heard of the shamans burned alive; some even knew them.

"Yes, Grantville has many Christians, they are mostly Christian, and this is the time of the year they celebrate their God's birth. But they are unlike the Christians we have met. They did not ask me to forget our ancestors or forget our ancestral ways. They do not want to burn people like Aikia here. Indeed, they banned witch burning in their lands. A giant up-timer once killed a witch-burner when he wouldn't stop, and he was lauded for it." The hissing stopped.

"They have a gift-giving avatar of their god who arrives for the birthday. He is said to live north of here. They call him Santa. As you can see, he is dressed for our land." Erik pulled out a stiff card with a picture of an old man, dressed in red and white furs and black boots. He didn't dress like anyone they knew. They preferred much more colorful clothing, but he looked like he knew the cold.

"He delivers gifts from his sleigh on the birth night, entering every believer's tent and lodge." Erik pulled out another stiff card, it showed a sleigh. The sleigh looked overloaded with sacks and too delicate for use, but maybe that didn't matter to the avatar of a god.

Erik paused for another sip of soup. He pulled another, larger card out of his pack. "See how his sleigh is pulled?"

The people were quiet as they looked over the card. The art on that card was different, the sleigh was flying through the air, and it was pulled by pairs of reindeer. The reindeer looked a little odd, but they were definitely reindeer. "Do you think a Swede could get pairs of reindeer to pull a sleigh through the air? Could a Dane do this, could a Russ? No, Santa must be one of us."

Natala

Iver P. Cooper

Kodachi Machi (Santa Cruz), Monterey Bay
November, 1634

"Hold up the child," said Yamaguchi Takuma. He dipped the pitcher into the water of the San Lorenzo River, then lifted it up again, a few droplets scattering as he did so. "I baptize thee Luis Goto, in the name of the Father and of the Son and of the Holy Ghost," he intoned as he poured the water over the infant's head.

Luis Goto cried in outrage. His mother started to apologize and Takuma laughed. "Don't worry, he isn't the first to cry, and he won't be the last."

Unlike any other baptism Takuma had conducted for his little group of *kirishitan* back in Japan, this one was attended by a *daimyo*. And not just any *daimyo*, but Date Masamune, the Grand Governor of New Nippon. The reason for his attendance was that this was the first infant baptism in New Nippon, as the Japanese settlement in western North America was called.

It was not, however, the first baptism in New Nippon. Date Masamune's sixth son, Munesane, had been baptized "David Date" in August, immediately after the First Fleet made landfall in what the up-time maps called Alsea Bay, Oregon. David Date was also present on this solemn occasion, as was his half-sister, Date Chiyo-hime.

As a special honor, David Date had agreed to serve as Luis Goto's *padrinho*—godfather. The Portuguese term implied that Luis would receive David Date's patronage.

David Date congratulated Luis Goto's parents and they introduced him to Luis' older brother, Sebastiao, who looked to be about seven years old. The boy hid behind his mother.

David smiled and said, "Please let me know if there is anything I can do for your family."

The mother and father looked at each other. "There is something you can do for us. Really, for our whole community," said the father.

David's eyebrows flickered. "Yes?"

"I know you were only just baptized, but you surely know that one of the two great holidays of our faith is almost upon us: Christmas. We would like to have a proper Christmas, with a mass and a feast and so on."

"But who would perform a mass?" asked David. "Isn't a priest needed? As far as I know, there are no priests in New Nippon. None came forward and surrendered themselves to the authorities."

"I thought—I thought that since in an emergency, any Christian can perform a baptism, that perhaps now, when there is no priest within ten thousand li, our *dojuku* could hold mass."

Imamura Yajiro, presently New Nippon's only *dojuku*—lay catechist—was standing nearby. He waved his hand back and forth in front of his face, a gesture of negation. "So sorry, only a priest may conduct the liturgy of the Eucharist. I can read the Gospel aloud and give sermons, that's all."

"That's fine for an ordinary day," said the father, "but Christmas should be special. It is among the holiest of holy days. We saved our bodies by coming here, but what of our souls?"

David Date stole a glance at his father. His expression hadn't changed much, but he was clearly getting perturbed. The Shogun, Tokugawa Iemitsu, wanted all of the *kirishitan* gone from Japan. Dead or in exile didn't much matter to him. But since Date Masamune was the Grand Governor of New Nippon, he would lose face if New Nippon failed. And failure was more likely if the *kirishitan* of the First Fleet did not encourage their fellows to follow in their footsteps. And plainly, they were concerned with their life spiritual as well as their life material.

"May I make a suggestion? asked Takuma. "What about a Christmas play? I haven't seen one for more than two decades, but they used to be a fixture of the season."

"An excellent idea!" said David Date. "That would make Christmas special, neh?"

The father agreed.

"We'll have a Christmas play on Christmas Eve, and a feast on Christmas Day. I'll arrange the feast, and as for the play—Yajiro, you and Takuma see to it!"

* * *

"We don't have a lot of time," muttered Yajiro. "Christmas is December 25 of the European calendar. By my calculation, that is day 20 of the eleventh month of the *Taiinreki*. And the tenth month has already begun."

"I was a child when I saw my one and only Christmas play," admitted Takuma. "That was in Nagasaki, before 1614, when the missionaries were expelled. After that we moved to the countryside, where it was easier to avoid detection. So I hope you know more about Christmas plays than I do."

Yajiro sighed. "I know that the first Christmas play performed in Japan was the story of Adam and Eve. That was in Bungo in 1560. Later they became more elaborate, with multiple acts, all based on stories from the Bible that would be familiar to the parishioners." He meant the stories that would appear in prayer books and catechisms, or retold in sermons, as the Bible had not been translated into Japanese, and few Japanese, even among the *dojuku*, had and could read Latin or Portuguese editions.

"Well, let's start with Adam and Eve," said Takuma, "and see how much time we have left when that piece is complete. It's better to have one complete act than a half-dozen incomplete ones."

"Agreed."

"You know the Bible best," said Takuma. "Can you write a script?"

"I can," said Yajiro. "Can you deal with finding actors, and people to make the costumes and scenery. We'll need musicians, too."

"I will try," said Takuma. "I know we have *shamisen* players here at Kodachi Machi. I've heard them practicing! We have carpenters, and the women certainly know how to sew. I don't know if any professional actors were taken up in the *bakufu*'s net."

"With enough sake on hand for the audience, it won't matter...."

* * *

Staging "The Story of Adam and Eve" in California was not without its difficulties. Obviously, they needed a tree to represent the Garden of Eden. And it had to be a tree that hadn't lost its leaves. Unless they wanted to present a tree with fake leaves, made out of silk or paper.

With the help of First-to-Dance, an Ohlone Indian who was a good friend of Date Chiyo-hime, they found a suitable tree on a dry slope. It was really more a shrub than a tree, but that was just as well since it would make it easier to transport to Kodachi Machi and place on stage. First-to-Dance told them that in a well-watered area, it could grow to over a hundred feet.

The tree had deep-green, lance-shaped, leathery leaves. First-to-Dance crushed one of the leaves for them, and it gave off a peppery scent.

The good news was that its fruit was ripe. The bad news was that it looked nothing like an apple as depicted in the prayer books. The sermons always described the apple as red, and this fruit was purple. At best it was a reddish purple.

Takuma considered finding someone to paint or dye the fruit red, but First-to-Dance told him not to bother, the fruit would be gone before Christmas. So they would have to hang artificial fruit on the tree. But at least they could make it a good copy of a European apple. So with that fruit hanging from the branches of a California Bay Laurel, they had a "Paradise Tree."

Then there was the problem of the Snake—Satan in serpent form. Takuma consulted with the local craftsmen and it seemed best to make a two-person costume based on the traditional depictions of the *tatsu*, the Japanese dragon that could take on a humanoid form. The actor in the head would be able to utter Satan's honeyed words, and the one in the tail, well, it wasn't a demanding role.

Several people volunteered to play Adam, the First Man. Takuma and Yajiro had them each read some of Adam's lines—which Yajiro kept changing. much to Takuma's irritation—and move about the stage. At last one of the fishermen was honored with the role.

Casting Eve turned out to be difficult. Women had been banned from appearing in *kabuki* in 1629. Any female role had to be performed by an *onnagata*, a female impersonator. But there was no *onnagata* among the *kirishitan* in Kodachi Machi, and none of the men wanted to be dressed up as a woman.

Without Eve, there wasn't much of a story. So Takuma had to ask for a female volunteer. Here again there was a problem. The reason women were banned from *kabuki* theater—which was started by an all-female troupe in 1603—was that the *bakufu* came to the conclusion that many of the performers were engaged in prostitution. So none of the women wanted to invite malicious gossip by appearing on stage. Takuma pointed out that this performance had a high moral purpose, so there could be no taint, but that argument wasn't enough to sway any of the women into volunteering. But at last Takuma persuaded one of the women that she could wear a mask, like those worn in *Noh*, to hide her identity.

Takuma and Yajiro argued for a while over who to recruit to play God. Yajiro said one of the samurai should be given the role. But Takuma objected. "It would be sacrilegious to have a non-Christian play God. The only samurai who has professed the Faith is David Date, and his father keeps him way too busy for him to learn his lines."

Fortunately, one of the other participants, who overheard the argument, came up with a solution: let God be heard but not seen. Then David Date could just read his lines, without having to memorize them. A craftsman designed a blind for David Date to stand behind. It would be equipped with a rolled-up *o uma jirishi*, a great standard, like that which accompanied a *daimyo* on the battlefield. When God was about to speak, David would cut a rope, and "God's standard," bearing a red cross on a white background, would unroll. And David would use a speaking trumpet to amplify his voice.

The final role was that of the angel. The angel would usher Adam and Eve out of Heaven, and then bar the path back to the Garden of Eden with his katana. The actor expressed some anxiety about this. "Only samurai are allowed to carry a katana, and I am not a samurai. One could charge the stage and behead me."

"We'll have you dress like a samurai, with a *kataginu* jacket and *hakama* trousers—"

'That will make them even more likely to behead me!" the actor complained.

"Let me finish. And you'll wear a mask, so no one knows your real identity. Or class."

"I suppose."

* * *

The next day, Takuma got nervous about the casting of the angel of the Garden, and decided to ask David Date for approval. He got even more nervous as he waited for David to finish his *iaijitsu* practice—*iaijitsu* was the art of combining the drawing of the katana with a slash at an opponent.

At last David Date motioned him forward. "How is the Christmas play coming along?"

"Fine, sir, but I have a question..." Takuma explained the problem.

"There's no problem, Takuma. Kabuki and Noh actors play samurai often enough, and they are commoners, too. But instead of a katana, an angel should have a *nodachi*." That was a great sword, with a blade three shaku long. The blade of a katana was no longer than two *shaku*.

"Where would I get one?"

"We have one in the armory. Nowadays, it is used for ceremonial purposes, not for fighting. You can't wear it on your waist, like a katana, but it can be placed in a back-sheath. I would suggest your actor practice carrying and drawing it."

"I am much obliged, my lord."

"Also...make sure the *hakama* are the everyday use kind that end a bit above floor level. If your actor tries wearing the ceremonial kind that trail behind your feet, he's likely to end up tripping himself. Which is an especially bad idea when holding a *nodachi*."

* * *

One day, the Grand Governor dropped by rehearsal. He watched and listened to the "Story of Adam and Eve," and then ordered Yajiro and Takuma to his office.

"But shouldn't we do another run through? Christmas is only—"

"Now!"

* * *

They had barely reached the audience room in the Kodachi Machi castle when he turned and confronted them, not even bothering to sit down on his *zabuton* cushion. "What were you thinking, choosing this particular story?"

"I am sorry, my lord," said Takuma, "I don't understand the problem. Adam and Eve are created. They come to the Garden of Eden. Eve is tempted by Satan and eats the apple from the tree of the knowledge of good and evil. God reprimands then, and an angel drives them out of Paradise. Then—"

"Stop there!" commanded Date Masamune. "Didn't it occur to either of you two idiots that the *kirishitan* were forced to leave Japan, just as Adam and Eve were forced to leave Paradise? Might they not equate Japan and Paradise? Do we want to remind them that they have lost Paradise?"

Takuma and Yajiro did the only thing they could do. They knelt and touched their foreheads to the floor.

After a moment or two, Date Masamune harrumphed and said, "Oh, get up, both of you! We—meaning you—need to fix this."

"Uh, what do you suggest, sir?"

"Can you leave out that story?"

"If we do, I am not surely we can have enough of a show ready by Christmas," said Takuma. "We aren't experienced dramatists, and our actors and musicians aren't professionals, either. As it is, we still need to come up with another act or two for the performance to be a reasonable length."

"Didn't you like the temptation scene, my lord?" asked Yajiro.

"Yes, yes. I don't suppose you could, oh, just have God give them a reprimand and tell them not to eat another apple?"

"I'm afraid not, sir. The audience would know better," said Takuma.

"I have an idea!" said Yajiro. "We could do an act about the Jews entering the Promised Land. Canaan."

"Hmm..." said Date Masamune. "All right. Make that the finale. And make sure the Promised Land looks like California."

December, 1634

The show was coming together. They had two acts, the "Story of Adam and Eve" and the "Story of Moses, Joshua, and the Promised Land."

'It's a pity that for our first Christmas play, we don't have a scene that actually features Jesus Christ," said Takuma.

"I know, I know," said Yajiro. "But you know why I picked Adam and Eve. And then we were ordered to end with the Promised Land. The parishioners' grasp on the Bible is shaky enough without putting Jesus in the middle of the play, out of chronological order. "

"Suppose we put a stable and a crib on stage, off in a corner, to symbolize the birth of Christ."

"How big a stage do you think we are going to have?"

"Well, there's the castle courtyard..."

"What if it rains? Or snows? We have to be able to perform indoors. And even if only the kirishitan from Kodachi Machi show up, that's at least five hundred people. "

"Okay, if we are indoors, we just use the crib. If we're outdoors, well, there's a stable off the courtyard, so we put the crib by it."

"I can live with that. When would you bring it on?"

"We just leave it there for the whole show."

Christmas Eve

"Jitters?" asked Takuma.

"I am sweating buckets," said Yajiro. "There are a bunch of samurai in attendance. I didn't expect that."

"You should have," said Takuma. "Plenty of samurai like kabuki, after all. There's not a lot of alternative entertainment in Kodachi Machi in December. And the free food and drink is also a draw."

"And what if those samurai, almost all of whom are not Christian, get drunk and then bored? If there's a ruckus, who will get punished? Not the samurai!"

"They won't dare make a ruckus with the Grand Governor and his family in attendance."

"I hope you're right."

* * *

At least, thought Takuma, the weather was acceptable, so they could use the castle courtyard. If they had been forced to move the show indoors, they would have had to have several showings to accommodate everyone who wanted to see it.

But even the courtyard was getting a bit crowded. Plainly, they had underestimated the demand for a Christmas play.

* * *

For musical accompaniment, they had the conch shells and drums that the samurai used for communication on the battlefield, a couple of *shamisen* and bamboo flutes, and a single *koto*. Their koto player was Date Chiyo-hime. However, as a gesture of respect for her status, she would play from behind a screen.

The first act was the Story of Adam and Eve. A conch shell was blown, and a curtain dropped revealing Adam, and then he took a bone out from under his shirt and dropped it behind the second curtain. That dropped, too, revealing Eve. Yajiro was the narrator, and his dialogue was accompanied by the *shamisen*.

The highlight of Act One was the Temptation. When Satan spoke to Eve, some of the playgoers burst into tears, and others yelled out, "Don't listen to him!"

As Eve reached for the apple, one of the musicians started drumming on a *taiko*, first slowly and then more quickly as her hand came closer. The conch shell was blown again as she took her first bite. And after Adam joined her, the bamboo flutes shrilled.

The serpent had some unfortunate difficulties with the slithering off part. The head got caught on something and the actor inside had to choose between tearing the costume and backing up. The backing up took the actor in the tail by surprise, and the tail moved about a bit spastically. But they managed to get off stage, albeit not without a few derogatory hoots from the audience.

Takuma held his breath when the angel drew his sword. In rehearsal, the angel had once drawn the sword a bit too forcefully and overbalanced. Fortunately, he did not cut himself or anyone else. He did however put a gouge in the *tatami* mat and Takuma first covered it up and then had it replaced on the sly. This time, however, the *nodachi* went where it was supposed to go. It gleamed in the afternoon sun, and Takuma liked how the angel held it, two-handed, to bar the path to the Garden.

Takuma and Yajiro had thought about coating the blade in oil and setting that on fire, to better duplicate the "flaming sword" of the Bible, but decided that would be pushing their luck too far.

After the first act, the stage hands quickly set up *jinmaku*. Those were the camp curtains used by the samurai when they were on the march. In front of the *jinmaku*, the masons who had directed the building of the castle came out and danced the *suzume odori*, the sparrow dance. This dance was in honor of Date Masamune, whose *mon* featured two sparrows. It had first been performed, in fact, by the masons who built his clan's home castle at Sendai.

The dance was in part to fill out the performance—two acts weren't much, but they hadn't had much time to put the play together—and in part to give time for set and costume changes. And of course buttering up the grand governor had its own advantages.

As the dancers twirled around and waved their fans, behind the *jinmaku*, the props and scenery from the first act were hastily moved out, and those for the second act moved in.

The dancers left the stage, and the *jinmaku* was dropped to the ground. On stage right was a large tablet, painted in a bronze color, and representing the Ten Commandments. In the center was a miniature stage, like that of the *bunraku*, the puppet theater. And on stage left was a miniature walled city, mounted on a cart.

The Lord told Moses that he would lead the Israelites out of Egypt to the promised land. The narrator talked about the plagues—Takuma and Yajiro hadn't figured out how to stage them. The pursuit of the Israelites by the Pharaoh's army, the parting of the waters, and the drowning of the pursuers was shown with puppets. The heads and costumes weren't as ornate as that of the *bunraku* but the *kirishitan* prop makers had done the best they could in the time available.

The forty years of wandering in the wilderness was condensed down to about forty seconds.

The cart was slowly wheeled out and twelve actors blowing on conch shells marched around it six times. Then they moved in front of the cart, blocking it from the audience's view, and when they backed away, the city had collapsed. (The city was made of little blocks, and they had given its base a good shake.)

"Behold," said the narrator, "the city of Jericho is fallen, and the Israelites enter the Promised Land."

A second *jinmaku* was carried onto the stage. The audience could see that this had been decorated with a reasonable likeness of Monterey Bay, as seen from a fishing junk.

* * *

The Grand Governor stood and clapped. Three times, three times, three times, and once. Then he repeated it. On the second time around, the whole audience joined in. The actors all came out, and bowed, even David Date.

Then the Grand Governor pointed at Takuma. He looked around, not realizing what was going on. His wife gave him a nudge and said, "Stand up and bow!" He did so.

* * *

Takuma and Yajiro were summoned a week later to the Grand Governor's audience chamber.

"Well done," he said. "I have presents for you."

They bowed ninety degrees. "Thank you, Masamune-dono."

"But there is a problem. The people in Kodachi Machi have been bragging about having gotten to see a Christmas play. It has made the kirishitan in Niji-Masu, Kawamachi and Andoryu envious. That is a bad thing.

"So for next year, you will have to stage Christmas plays there, too."

Takuma and Yajiro exchanged looks. There was only one possible answer. "Yes. my lord."

* * *

After they left the audience chamber, Yajiro turned to Takuma. "So, it appears we are now in show business."

* * *

Author's note: *Natala* was the period Japanese Christian term for Christmas. See Suter, *Holy Ghosts: The Christian Century in Modern Japanese Fiction* 78 (2015). It is derived from Latin *natalis*, birthday, and in context refers to the birth of Christ.

A Christmas Stollen

Edith Wild

Grantville High School

1636

The bell rang as Amalia skidded into the locker room. She rushed over to her assigned locker. She quickly undid her padlock, opened her locker, pulled out her PE uniform and sneakers. Amalia placed them on the bench that ran between the rows of lockers. It amused her that these lockers were a sort-of-green but the chipped paint was evidence of long use.

The locker room was getting emptier by the second. Amalia leaned over, took off her boots, then quickly got out of her school clothes. She was careful with her boots and jeans when she stuffed everything else into the locker.

Her boots were white Doc Martens "combat" style with red roses painted on the leather. The jeans, which her mother grumbled about, were lined with flannel to help keep her warm. Both were some rich up-timer extras that had been passed around several times. Her mother worked hard to pay for them. This deliberate masquerade was a habit, to show no evidence of extra money that was not explainable.

Amalia reached for her blue uniform shorts. The striped shirt slid off the bench and onto the floor. She rolled her eyes, tugging on the shorts. As Amalia pulled on her shirt over her head, something dropped, plopped, and made a little noise.

She looked around after she pushed her head out of the neck hole of her shirt. She didn't see anything out of place, then realized something was missing. She looked at her locker, then to the floor. Amalia blinked. They'd just been there. "Where are my sneakers? Who took them?"

"Ha! You'll be late!" Kunigunda laughed a couple meters away, struggling into her own uniform. "You can't beat me!"

"Screw it, you goose!" Amalia ran for the door, burst out of the locker room, and raced across the gymnasium floor in her socks. She got to the sweet spot where the floor was over-polished, skidded out into a twirl, and did not fall this time. Amalia whooped, facing her. "I beat you, Kunigunda!"

Kunigunda's face had an odd red mark near her mouth, the sort which would leave a bruise. She covered it with her hand, stifled a giggle. "You still don't have your sneakers!"

Amalia sighed. *It was going to be that way, huh?*

The rest of the PE classmates were neatly lined up in rows by then, about forty of them. Amalia slid into place in the back row. She noticed Maggie chattering with Ruthie and the new girl.

Mrs. Sims, the PE teacher, held a large ball in her other hand. She blew her whistle. "Listen up, team A and team C, you are up first. Notice the net! Everyone has to watch. Amalia, you are the first sub for team C—wait, where are your sneakers?"

"I don't know, Mrs. Sims." Amalia shrugged.

"See me after school tomorrow."

"Yes, ma'am." Amalia signed the slip. She stopped listening. Mrs. Sims was just taking attendance in her stupid little notebook. PE was just weird but the up-timers thought it important. Somehow being dressed differently or wrong meant getting a zero in participation for the day. Amalia was here, wasn't she?

Amalia sat on the bench on the right, so she'd cheer and yell at the players, faking her team spirit. She would get put in the game soon enough, would need to play nicely and not be mean. Being mean could get her another after-school detention.

It was disgusting, the way she was treated by everyone. Amalia was almost seventeen, not a child. She should be working and supporting her family, but no, that was not allowed by her parents. They had moved to Grantville three years ago to continue her father's training and for the high school.

At that moment she hated Kunigunda. She hated Mrs. Sims. And she hated volleyball most of all. Pointless. This was a waste of time.

* * *

Much later, after the last bell, Amalia left Grantville High School. The book sack slung over her shoulder was full and heavy. In the shadows created by the high school, the snow covering the grass looked somewhere between ankle and shin deep. *At least it's not raining or snowing*, Amalia thought. It was breezy though. She pulled her blue wool wrap tighter as she looked for her bus in the line of waiting buses. All showing wear. All labeled with *Calvert High School*. Amalia didn't get that. It was Grantville High School. No one ever called it anything else. Behind the buses were the horse-drawn carts and the occasional car.

She found her bus and got on. The bus was warmer than it was outside. Its heater worked. The engine was, as usual, painfully loud. Some students were shouting at each other in the back. Someone had dropped a window open and was yelling out at another bus. Amalia rolled her eyes. They were so childish, squawking at each other like birds.

A few minutes later, the buses started leaving the school's grounds. The ride to her stop thankfully wasn't long.

Stepping from the bus into the noise to Main Street, Amalia hurried into Rupert the Butcher's. It was on Water Street, near the bridge. She stood in line and picked up her mother's usual order, everything tidy and wrapped in brown paper, then walked the blocks to home.

Their home was in the apartment building on the southeastern corner of Clarksburg and Pleasant, across the street from a Baptist Church. The church was enormous, seemingly older than most of the other buildings in Grantville. Their apartment was a third-floor walk-up over some shops on the ground floor. It had a glass door to a vestibule that had mailboxes, and a second glass door that kept cold air out of the lobby and stair hall. Amalia climbed up the stairs all the way to the top floor.

She unlocked and opened the door. It was a small place, but it was home.

It was just Amalia and her mother. Neither her father nor her older brother, Heinrich, were home. They hadn't been for a long time. Her father had been away with the army in Magdeburg for nearly a year. As of the last letter, he was training to be a surgeon. And that letter was two months old, read to worn out. Heinrich was north and east with the army. He was a jäger with the Thuringian Rifles, usually beyond the main movements of men and machines. Amalia didn't pretend to follow war or politics; those things agitated her mother and were just bad news.

Amalia hung her wrap up on her peg by the front door and dropped her book bag on the well-worn couch in the sitting room. Between the dining and sitting areas sat the Swedish tile wood stove. Thankfully, the baseboard heaters appeared to be working, so she didn't need to light it.

Amalia took the brown paper package from Rupert's to the one-wall-style kitchen. She put it down on the wood counter next to the up-time "retro" fridge-freezer that they'd been lucky to get with the apartment. She opened the paper package and sorted through it, reading the labels.

There was a split chicken, each half in its own package. One half she left on the counter; the other half went into the freezer. Both pieces of the expensive beef to the freezer, too. The eggs, butter, dried fruits, even a tiny bit of candied orange peel from Italy, and a small bit of marzipan from Magdeburg went into the fridge.

Dinner tonight bore some consideration. Her mother had to be tired of the usual. Amalia got the big cast-iron pan out, plunked it on the stove, and lit the stove. From the pantry, she got out a bottle of beer and the home-canned peas. She pulled out the sharpest knife, a large bowl, and the wooden cutting board, putting them on the counter by the stove. She grabbed an onion from the bowl by the fridge, and sliced it thin. The pan was hot enough, so she put in the bacon fat.

Amalia put the chicken skin side down with a bit of salt, the sliced onion, and some sprigs of rosemary from the herb-pot on the kitchen window sill. She turned and grabbed a turnip and a few carrots, parsnips, and potatoes, and then scrubbed them clean. Amalia cut them all into bite-sized pieces, putting them in the large bowl off to the side.

She carefully flipped the chicken over. The skin looked crispy enough. She added the other vegetables except the canned peas to the pot around the chicken.

While dinner was cooking, Amalia tidied the apartment. Moved the stuff that somehow migrated out of her bedroom back into her bedroom. Swept, then damp mopped the floor in the main living area. Glanced into the bathroom, it looked clean enough. Occasionally she went to the kitchen and moved the vegetables around the pot so they wouldn't get too brown. Pretty soon the apartment was warm and fragrant with the scent of good food. Amalia washed the dishes and flatware she used, leaving them all in the drying rack.

She went back to the stove. Dinner looked good so far, so she poured in a cup of beer. As she scraped the brown bits off the bottom of the pot, Amalia could almost hear her mother say the brown was flavor and not to waste it. She wiped down the countertops. She stirred dinner again, added in the canned peas, then turned it down to low-simmer.

Amalia glanced at the clock. It was just after 4:30 PM. Her mother would be home soon and be tired from working in the lawyer's office all day. She wanted a solid dinner ready so her mother could eat and explain the expensive candied orange peel. Amalia flicked the lights on in advance of sunset. She dragged out her "homework" out of her book sack. She'd been avoiding it this week. Math was never an issue, nor was science, or what passed for history.

The book for English class was small, scarcely a hundred pages or so. It was a well-made book, a reprint, bound in red leather, dainty pages, small black letters. The title was in English of course, *A Christmas Carol by Charles Dickens.*

"Where's my placeholder? Which stave am I in?" Amalia whispered as she shifted the pages. She'd not looked at the little book in a couple of days. She dumped her book sack out. Nothing. She'd left some markers in there, but really hadn't paid much attention. She thought about it. The only person who ever paid attention...Well, no one. Not since Heinrich left. Kunigunda wouldn't touch this either.

Stave III, "The Second of the Three Spirits," didn't look right, she decided, turning the delicate pages. Three pages in, it started looking familiar. Her mother's locket fell out from where it had been pressed in the book.

Amalia frowned. Why wasn't it in her mother's jewelry box? How did it end up there?

The apartment's doorbell rang from the lobby downstairs. The "intercom" still actually worked, as the jokes about some technology ran around Grantville. A familiar voice shouted into the intercom, "I'm here! Let me in!"

"Maggie? What are you doing here?"

"I'll tell you when I see you!"

Amalia buzzed Maggie in. Maggie always took forever on the stairs. She put the kettle on. It was cold enough outside to want to be nice and offer tea.

A few minutes later, there was a knock on the door. Amalia opened it to let Maggie in.

In perfect English, Maggie said, "Oh, it smells so good here. It makes me envy your dinner!"

Maggie took off her wrap and hung it up on the peg next to Amalia's. Her wrap was a dark gray with lighter gray flowers embroidered on the edge. Her cap came off too, letting out a halo of mouse-brown curls. It was growing back from having been burnt to a crisp in a botched experiment with a wonky old curling iron a few months back. Maggie sat down at the kitchen table. "It is so cold out. Do you have tea?"

"Yes. The kettle is on." Amalia spoke cheerfully, also in perfect English. She got out the tea box and two silvery tea balls. Filled the balls with tea. Amalia opened the cupboard next to the sink, pulling out two large up-time mugs: one green and one white with black cats on it. She filled the tea-balls and put one in each mug. "It'll be a few minutes. What's going on?"

Without missing a beat, Maggie said, "So you don't know?"

"Know what? Did something finally happen to Kunigunda for being such a jerk to me every single day this week?" Amalia asked.

Maggie coughed. "Well, Petronella caught her and Leo Halvorson. She smacked her in the face for messing with her boyfriend."

"I saw Kunigunda right after. Her face was so red. I heard that Petronella smacked Leo, too." Amalia said, smiling a little from schadenfreude. Leo was such a sleaze. She guessed Petronella and Leo were off again, the fourth time since last spring. Amalia didn't know what Petronella saw in him that made him so great. Why did she forgive Leo all the time for stupid things he did that hurt her?

"Kunigunda thinks you saw her smooching Leo Halvorson."

"I did not! How could I? Meike told me what happened at lunch." Amalia interrupted, horrified. Ugh, why would she want to see that? That time a few months ago when she walked in on Leo messing around with another girl was enough.

"And she thinks you told Petronella beforehand that Leo was going to kiss her."

"Wait, does that mean that Kunigunda and Leo did this more than once?" Amalia asked. She had no proof, but Leo must have lied to Kunigunda about who knows what, or how many times. And like a gullible fool that girl believed him and acted on those lies. Suddenly, this week made sense. Amalia felt her anger rise like a knife. Boys were so dumb. "Because of Kunigunda, I got an after-school detention! My mother is going to be so upset with me."

The kettle shrieked. Amalia was glad for the interruption, needing to get away from the conversation. She poured the hot water over the tea balls in the cups, and put the kettle on a trivet. "It'll be three minutes. Do you want honey?"

"Honey is good. I'm sorry, I didn't mean to upset you." Maggie picked up her tea mug, the green one, stirred at her tea, bobbling the metal tea ball, settling quietly at the table. "You know my mom sells tickets at the train station."

"Well, yes. She's done that for a few years." Amalia went to get the honey from the pantry, glad to charge the topic. "What about it?"

"Your mom bought a ticket to Magdeburg." Maggie hesitated. "This morning. One ticket. Both to and from. Round-trip."

"What?" Amalia felt the blood drain from her face. She sat down on the wood chair. The world stopped making sense.

Maggie looked unhappy, reached into a pocket. "Your mom wrote you a note."

"Give it." Amalia reached for the letter.

Maggie gently placed the folded paper in her hand.

"When did you get this?" Amalia unfolded it. On the top right-hand corner was today's date, 11th of December, 1636.

"I've only had it for about two hours." Maggie bit her lip and continued, "I was going to meet you here earlier, but my mom needed help at her window at the train station so she could close up."

"When did your mom get this?" Amalia asked.

"My mom said she's had it since late this morning. Your mom talked to my mom. Then your mom explained she got a telegram."

"Oh?"

"Not a normal telegram but a finance one. It had a one seventy-five credit line from Thurn und Taxis in it for one round-trip ticket to Magdeburg and a hotel room there. Oh, and meals for two weeks."

"Ok. How long will it take to get there?"

Maggie thought for a few seconds. "Ten hours including stops at this time of year."

"But she's gone for two weeks?" Amalia put down the note on the table. She got up again. She retrieved the honey jar from the pantry and grabbed two spoons and a small plate for the tea balls. "I suppose I should read it."

"Sixteen days, unless she changes her mind. My mom said you aren't supposed to read it alone." Maggie asked, "What does it say?"

Maggie removed the tea ball from her mug. Amalia did the same.

Amalia picked up the note. Her mother's handwriting was messier than her usual clear cursive. Thankfully it was still legible. "Listen, then." She read it aloud:

Dear Ama,

Do not read this alone. Maggie is a good soul and will be there for you, as I am afraid I do not know her mother well but I know Maggie somewhat and I know you know her. I received three telegrams this morning. The news is good and bad.

The first telegram I received was from your Aunt Lucia. She is coming for Christmas and will be staying at The Higgins Hotel in Grantville from December 13th to January 2nd. She is bringing Rolf von Leuthold with her, her husband's sister's oldest son.

You are going to have dinner with them on the 13th. Be aware, she is fussy. She's a very great lady! Be ready. Wear your lemon yellow silk frock. You may borrow a piece or two of my jewelry.

"You have an aunt who's *adel*?" Maggie interrupted, sounding impressed.

"Not important, just a fairy-godmother type." Amalia frowned. Last time Aunt Lucia had visited them was about four years ago when they were still living in Jena. So this was a little unusual. She wondered why Maggie needed to be here for news like this.

"You have a fairy-godmother?" Maggie laughed a bit, slightly distracted. "That's cute. Funny."

Amalia made a face, but continued reading aloud.

The second telegram was from your father. He related that he is well. But Heinrich was thrown from his horse and is in the hospital in Magdeburg. His right leg was badly broken at his knee.

Amalia had to pause to breathe. Her heart was in her throat. Here, the pen's ink bloomed like watercolor flowers from a couple of dried tears. Amalia touched them with her fingertips. Her mother hardly ever cried. She must have been so afraid.

Heinrich was immediately attended to by the duke's own doctor. He did not amputate—

Amalia's heart felt like it stopped for a moment. Her voice shook. She blinked away tears.

—and he felt the leg may yet be saved. As an army surgeon-in-training, your father volunteered to go with Heinrich to the hospital in Magdeburg.

Amalia imagined Heinrich's agony and felt ill. She couldn't imagine how her mother managed to write this note.

The doctors at the hospital did something called an x-ray to look at the bones. His right femur is broken in a few pieces, as well as something called a tibial plateau and a thing called a meniscus, which has rolled up. Your father said surgery to put Heinrich's leg back together is scheduled for later today. The surgeon was trained by Doctor Nichols in the 'art' of reconstruction.

The third telegram had the credit line from Thurn und Taxis, the banking house people your father hates to deal with. I do not know where your father got the money for the credit line from.

Even so, I am boarding the train to Magdeburg in a few minutes. I hope to be with your father and brother soon. I will send news when I can.

I love you. Take care please,

Then her mother signed off at the bottom of the note.

Amalia's heart hurt. She clung for composure to keep on a brave face. She wasn't sure if it worked. She couldn't look at Maggie. The conversation only lasted a few more minutes, just idle chit-chat about school, before it grew unbearably awkward.

Maggie left. Amalia locked the door behind her. She had declined the dinner invite. And, honestly, Amalia was relieved that Maggie had. She wasn't really a friend or ally, but she was not a problem either, really. They had shared some classes, and even had worked on a couple group projects together, but not in the last year. Maggie seemed not to want to be obligated. She simply did a favor and nothing more.

Amalia put the used dishes in the sink. Dumped out Maggie's half-drunk tea mug. Emptied out the drying rack. Cleaned the tea balls. Half-heartedly washed the plate, the mug, then the spoons.

A small sob escaped her control. Amalia noticed her hands were trembling. She glanced out the window, and saw Maggie's form in the light from the streetlights walking back to Main Street and the bus loop. The wind had picked up, blowing from the north. Storm was coming, and she could feel it. She breathed in, then out several times.

Amalia served herself some dinner and went back to the little table. She sat down and couldn't ignore the three empty chairs or the silence. She poked at her cut-up chicken and vegetables. Her appetite was gone, distant. She got up and put away the leftovers, which was most of it, for tomorrow. Put the honey jar back in the pantry.

Amalia sat down on the couch. In a terrible way, she felt grateful that her mother didn't like putting up Christmas decorations before the 15th of December. The idea of celebrating now felt awful. She put her face into her hands. And wept.

It was all ruined. Her worst nightmare was now real. Her father told her enough times when she was younger to keep a low profile and don't make too many waves. A bit of attention was fine, but too much was dangerous. That kind of thing. Amalia knew down to her bones that their invisibility was a precious thing. And it was gone.

Without a doubt, Maggie would tell her mother everything tonight. The adel thing would come out, and soon enough it would be everywhere. Then there would be obligations and more.

They lived without it for five years. Amalia could remember the lessons for stuff she was supposed to know, but only just. Her tutors had been old-fashioned and very strict. It had been so lonely. She didn't like thinking about it.

Amalia got up, went to the bathroom, blew her nose, and cleaned her face. The cold water felt good. A glance in the mirror showed her that her eyes looked red. She looked away.

Amalia tried to do her precalculus homework, and it wasn't happening. It made no sense, which was weird because it was one of her favorite subjects. *Maybe I'm just tired*, she thought.

Her eyes caught the book, *A Christmas Carol*. Amalia reached for the little red covered novel and began reading the stave, "The Second of the Three Spirits." Her head felt very heavy, but the book did keep her interest this time. The last line she read was, *"'I am the Ghost of Christmas Present,' said the Spirit. 'Look upon me.'"*

Amalia opened her eyes. The clock hanging on the wall said it was 6:00 AM. No sense of time had passed between evening and morning. Somehow it was over ten hours later. She got off the couch, drank some water from the kitchen tap, and blinked slowly. Her brain felt a bit foggy.

Amalia passed the calendar. It was Friday, 12th of December, 1636. Dread filled her. The quiz in English on *A Christmas Carol* was today. And she hadn't finished her homework. Amalia felt like crying, but didn't have the time. She screamed into a pillow instead, then she went to get ready for school.

Her reflection in the bathroom mirror was terrible. She looked sick, like she'd cried in her sleep, her hazel eyes puffy. She was blotchy. She rinsed her face with some water to get dried tears off and pulled on her school clothes.

It was colder outside today than yesterday. The air smelled like snow. By some miracle Amalia didn't miss the bus.

Upon reflection after getting to school, she decided that, if anything, it was a major miracle. She hadn't really looked where she was going, just put one foot in front of the other. Did she eat breakfast?

Her first class was English. A quiz on the stave for *A Christmas Carol* was passed around along with a Scantron sheet. She'd heard there were four of those machines in the building, which meant someone was maintaining those and making new Scantron sheets. And new inks. Just another weird thing up-timers did.

The quiz was twenty questions long. Amalia read them, bubbled in the circles, guessing on half of them. She worried about precalculus and that test, which was her next class. Quadratics.

But Mr. Lobkowitz was not there. The sub, Mr. Rothrock, did not have the test sheets, and he was only there until noon. So he called a drill and pushed the test to Monday, December fifteenth, the last possible day, two days before midterms. Yuck, studying for that would be a pain.

The rest of the day passed. Amalia ate by herself at lunch, not because she felt like eating, but because she didn't want to stand out. It felt like everyone was staring at her.

In PE, her sneakers had yet to be found. Kunigunda was unrepentant. Mrs. Sims gave her a scolding to be more careful, then gave her a pair of sneakers from the loner box for the following week. Amalia thought, they smell like summer feet! After class was done, she took them off and put them in her locker anyway.

Detention passed quickly, Amalia read through it, and didn't remember any of it afterwards. She hurried to the late bus to go home, to get away.

Her family's apartment was quiet and as warm as summer from the wall-board heaters. But the warmth didn't touch her. Not really.

Amalia reheated some of last night's dinner on the stove. Leftovers went back into the fridge. She sat at the kitchen table, and stared at her bowl of fragrant steaming food. She looked to the beer, but drank some more water instead.

The note was still sitting on the table. Amalia cried, head in hands, for a long time. Her poor brother was hurt. Her mother left her behind. She didn't remember if she said anything to anyone, except maybe to Mrs. Sims. The longer the school day had gone on the more whispers had followed her.

Why hadn't her mother pulled her out of school, so Amalia could go too? Amalia didn't have to be here for Aunt Lucia. Grantville was so different from anywhere else that plenty of people came to holiday here. Aunt Lucia could easily entertain herself and her nephew, Rolf von Leuthold. Amalia didn't want to think about the dinner with them tomorrow.

And why had her mother said for Maggie to be there with Amalia when she read the letter in the first place? Maggie must have said something to a friend or two at school, and Maggie's friends weren't that discreet. Or someone overheard Maggie saying something. This news was too juicy and too new to not pass along.

After a while, Amalia made herself eat. It went slowly. She could barely taste it. She washed up everything after. The middle school's bells rang from the next block over, marking the time. It was jarring to hear the sound of Christmas carols, sleds and bells on horse harnesses, laughter, voices, echoed up from the street below. They sounded so happy.

Amalia curled in the great overstuffed chair by the window to read Stave 3, "The Second of the Three Spirits," in *A Christmas Carol*. It opened with Scrooge dumbfounded, in the midst of a snore. The character—seemingly, if only to confront the next spirit—was glad to be awake. Amalia thought Scrooge evil and oily to that point, concerned really only with money. It was familiar, similar in a way.

The memory of it was old, faint from time, but Amalia remembered overhearing her father arguing with his grandfather and his father. Getting into Leahy Medical for physician training rotation was her father's dream. The medical school in Jena was a passageway. He hadn't wanted to be seen as depending on his natural rights of status by anyone, but by qualifying through merit. Either because they didn't understand it or just didn't want him to go, they didn't support her father's plan. Loudly. Her mother or Heinrich had tried to keep her away from it, she thought. And Amalia wasn't sure if the argument had happened more than once either.

Whatever the result was, when Amalia was eleven and Heinrich was fourteen, her parents had moved them to Jena. Both her parents seemed happier there than they were before. The medical school in Jena provided the opportunity for her father to make his dream a reality. He had been accepted and, as far Amalia knew, he did quite well there.

Amalia shook her head. Her eyes had roamed the page, but she hadn't taken anything in. She started from the top of the page. After a time, the words on the page sucked her in. Amalia disconnected from the world, forgot her problems. A sense of unreality permeated everything. The Ghost of Christmas Present took Scrooge to Tiny Tim's home. There was a total poverty of material things but there was wealth in the love which was so obvious it hurt.

At some point she must have drifted into sleep, since Amalia awoke suddenly at about 1:00 AM still curled up in the overstuffed chair. She could have sworn Heinrich was sitting on the sofa across from her. He seemed to be looking at her, looking around. A concerned expression was on his face.

"Heinrich," she whispered. She wiped her face. It was wet with tears.

His figure seemed to say no, his mouth opened and closed. Words, maybe? His voice wasn't reaching her ears.

"No to what?" Amalia whispered.

Then he was gone as if he'd never been there. It had to be a dream.

Stiffly she unfolded herself from her chair and rubbed her legs. Her feet felt tingly then the feeling spread everywhere and vanished. Amalia stood and stared at the couch. It looked like the sofa held an indentation, but that was not possible.

She shivered, made her way to her bedroom, and shut her door. Her bed was crammed into a corner across from a big window. She'd not slept in it for two days. Amalia stripped off her clothes, pulled on her soft woolen nightgown, and climbed into bed. It was cold, but warmed up quickly.

This time sleep gave no dreams, at least none she remembered.

The morning light woke her, as did a sound. A pebble on glass. Many times.

Amalia rose up, moved the curtain out of the way to peek out the window. The sky was a bright blue. The road below looked both icy and windswept. Traffic looked about the usual amount for mid-morning on a Saturday.

Parked in front of her building was a carriage, a nice one with two horses and a driver. Three people standing there looked up. They were in great warm cloaks. One of which was a richly decorated light blue. The other was black. The last one was dark gray—*Maggie's? What is Maggie doing with my aunt?* They apparently saw her move the curtain, looked back at each other, and seemed to have a short discussion. They disappeared below where the lobby was.

Amalia threw on fresh clothes, white brocade jeans and a silky shirt. She pulled on the red sloppy sweater she'd stolen from Heinrich just before he left. She felt like he was hugging her, needing the comfort of it today. Amalia quickly finger-combed her light brown hair, braided it, and tied the end with a bit of black ribbon. She twirled her braid into a bun, so the ribbon's bow was underneath, then pinned it in a few places to keep it in place. She slipped her red house slippers onto her feet.

As she closed her bedroom door behind her, Amalia heard Maggie shout over the intercom, "Can we come up?"

"Yes, you can." Amalia buzzed them into the inner lobby. She gently inspected her hair with her fingers. It felt like it looked okay. Hopefully it didn't look like a bird's nest.

She glanced at the time on the stove. It was 9:29 in the morning. She had perhaps three or four minutes. Amalia wondered how Maggie was distracting them to slow them down this much, then decided she didn't care. She tried to remember the court's social niceties, and panicked a little when she couldn't. It had been too long. Tea was probably a good start though.

Amalia put the tea kettle on the stove to boil. She set four matching tea cups out, the nice yellow floral ones, and filled the teapot's silvery tea ball with enough loose-leaf green tea for eight cups. She grabbed the honey jar, then found the lemon cookies from Di Camillo's Bakery and plated those with a pretty china plate. Amalia put it all on the nice tray her mother had gotten from an estate sale last summer.

There was a knock on the front door. She hurried over, unlocked, and opened the door.

"Good morning, Tante Lucia, Cousin Rolf, and my friend Maggie." Amalia spoke modestly, mostly toward the older woman, and curtsied slightly. She must have looked incongruous in jeans, a sweater, and house slippers. Nothing she could do about it now.

Tante Lucia swept in, barely acknowledging any courtesies. She was a stately woman with perfectly coiffed dark gray hair. Her elegant jewels and formal travel dress looked odd in the somewhat shabby apartment. She was followed by the others. Amalia closed the door.

"It is late in the day already. Your parents are not here? But in Magdeburg. Yes, your friend Maggie has told us," *Tante* Lucia spoke in court French.

"I did not know you would be here so soon, Tante Lucia. I, I did not mean to oversleep," Amalia said, trying to hide the wince when she realized she had been speaking in English. She could read and understand court French just fine, but was terrible at speaking it. Worse, she couldn't remember when she had practiced it last either.

Tante Lucia frowned at her, ignoring the apology, said in accented English, "This apartment is tiny and plain." She took off her gloves, holding them in one hand. "How much space do you actually have?"

The tea kettle chose at that moment to whistle. Amalia went to the kitchen and took it off the burner. She wished her mother were here. Her mother spoke perfect court French and was better at communicating with the upper-class relatives. At least the bathroom and bedroom doors were shut, thank goodness for small flavors. Since Amalia had already put her foot in it twice already, she continued speaking in English, "Not a lot, but enough. We don't need that much space."

She kind of remembered the wing of the *Gutshaus* in which her family had lived. What was its name? Oh, *Winterheim*. It was large. Stern paintings of ancestors. Gilded in public spaces. Busy with servants at all hours.

Little privacy. The grounds were acres and acres big. To be honest, Amalia hadn't missed it.

"Your father could have chosen any good house here. He has the money." *Tante* Lucia said, keeping in English as well.

"What money?" Amalia said as she poured water into the teapot. The tea only needed a minute or two to steep. Her parents were frugal. So what?

Her aunt didn't answer, gave an intense look, and just asked, "Is the tea ready?"

"Yes, I think so." Amalia took the tea ball out, brought the tray of tea and cookies out to the coffee table.

The conversation meandered from there. It felt awkward, like a dance that she didn't know the steps for. The lemon cookies vanished. Another pot of tea was drawn. Amalia got out the marzipan- filled cookies with a raspberry glaze. A third pot of tea came and went. It was nearly lunchtime when *Tante* Lucia and Rolf finally left.

Rolf had stayed quiet the entire time, sipping hot tea, eating cookies, and looking preoccupied. He mostly stared at the bookshelf. Her father's textbooks were there. Amalia hoped that she hadn't been rude to him by speaking a language that Rolf didn't understand. Surely *Tante* Lucia would've said something if that were the case? But she did tell Amalia that she'd paid the landlord for the apartment next door. Maggie would be staying there, so that she would have a companion and no possible scandal, until her mother came back from Magdeburg, if not longer.

Amalia rubbed her forehead. She didn't know who would cause a scandal with her and didn't want to. But she'd already told her mother that, on top of none of them being in the right social class, the boys at Grantville High School weren't that interesting to her. She found it off-putting when so many of them acted childishly or, worse, recklessly rode motorcycles.

The studious ones were okay, good study partners at the school's library. Staying away and ignoring all of them was easier.

Amalia knew her father was waiting until after she finished her education before doing any serious matchmaking. She wasn't too worried about it. Her father was a good man. She knew he would take her opinions seriously. Her mother's input would be important to him, too.

The footman from the carriage brought up Maggie's trunk. He unlocked the connecting door to the apartment next door, and then he left too.

Amalia and Maggie went inside together. It was smaller than Amalia's apartment by over half at least. There was a main room, a bedroom, and a bathroom. It was fully furnished, but none of the apartments in this building came that way. All of the furniture must have been moved in yesterday while she was at school. Her after-school detention gave them more time to finish without her noticing. Money and status greased a lot of wheels.

Across from the window in the main room, there was a large cupboard bed. It smelled like the wood sealer might be still drying. Something of its size had to have been made locally, probably at Rudolstadt. Next to the front door was a tight kitchen, about a meter in length. In the bedroom, smaller than Amalia's, was Maggie's bed, shoved against the wall.

"You are here to stay? She had you set up while we were talking?"

"That's what your aunt said, 'Set Maggie up, no young lady should be alone like this.' This is your mother's idea originally, not mine, or my mother's." Maggie exhaled. "I have a telegram for you from this morning. Your mother said it was private, so your aunt didn't see it."

"Ok." Amalia sat next to Maggie.

Maggie pulled it out from her pocket, and handed it to Amalia. She didn't know if she wanted to read it. She opened it and read it aloud.

Dear Ama,

Your father and I have not left Heinrich's bedside. We almost lost Heinrich last night. Your brother stopped breathing. It was about 1:00 AM, maybe before.

Your father knew what to do. I could only watch. The room was filled up with medical people then. They cracked his ribs with their CPR. At one point your father was breathing life into Heinrich's lungs and wouldn't quit.

The priest came and did the last rites. After some moments, Heinrich opened his eyes and whispered, "Amalia, Amalia, I cannot leave you!" Then he passed out. The doctors say it is a good sleep, not a coma.

God gave him back to us.

The fever has not broken. He is sleeping. His heart and lungs are fine. The swelling in his knee is ordinary for after the injury and surgery. A doctor drained the knee. Did you know bone marrow is greasy looking and red?

We have decided that you should not be alone at this time. Tante Lucia agreed to let the apartment next to ours, through that odd door that is always locked in our vestibule, and is putting Maggie in with you. Aunt Lucia's housekeeper, Frau Hummel, came with her and will live-in with you until the New Year or until we can move Heinrich.

Ich werde dich immer lieben,

deine Mutti

Amalia burst into tears, leaned on Maggie. Maggie put an arm around her. Amalia trembled. Her strange dream hadn't been one. Her brother had been here. She had seen him. And he had seen her. Amalia couldn't sort it, couldn't understand.

* * *

It was the 17th of December, 1636, a Wednesday. There were mid-term exams all week. Amalia had already taken the tests in chemistry, precalculus, and history. She was dreading the French test tomorrow. But English was today.

Amalia knew the English midterm was one hundred questions long, and twenty of them were going to be on *A Christmas Carol*, different questions from the quiz last week. It would have multiple choice and fill-ins. Tuesday had been the essay portion of the test. The teacher had a reading pulled from a novel and then had them write an essay on a singular question with several tasks. They'd practiced extensively. It was still very hard.

On the door to her English classroom was the list of the essay grades by student number. Amalia knew the point value was 9 and that the essay was 20 percent of the exam's grade. It looked like half of the students had passed the essay. She looked down the list until she saw her number. Out of 9, she got a 6. It wasn't terrible, a B.

Amalia took a deep breath, went in, and took the test.

Afterwards, Maggie sat next to her on the bus. Once off at the loop in downtown, they walked back to the apartment. The awkwardness hadn't left.

Maggie finally spoke. "I passed the essay. I got a 5."

"I passed too," Amalia said. She didn't want to hurt Maggie's feelings, or seem like she was bragging about getting a better grade.

"Is it true that those who get 4 or less will be dropped from Honors?"

"Not from one essay, I think. It is your whole merit."

Maggie wondered, "What university is going to take a woman?"

"The technical and teaching schools, Prague, even Jena in some programs."

"Ah. I'd forgotten that."

Maggie was silent for a few minutes, by which time the bus got to their stop on Main Street. They turned the corner at Main and Market. They walked as fast as possible, which given the icy sidewalks, wasn't very fast. They hurried past Rupert the Butcher's, DiCamillo's Italian Bakery, and the Villareals' Rock Shop. It was so gusty Amalia thought she'd freeze solid before they went across the bridge. She said so, a bunch of times, to Maggie.

The bridge was worse. The wind felt colder, like it was trying to throw them off of it.

Once in the small lobby, Amalia counted the stairs, sixteen per floor. Maggie slowly followed as always.

"You're limping?" Amalia asked.

Maggie didn't reply and kept climbing.

Amalia bit her lip. "Well?"

"I can't bound up these steps like a deer, not like you. It's no big deal."

Amalia turned around on the landing. "Have you always been like this?"

"Can we talk upstairs?"

"Sure." Like always Amalia was at the top waiting for Maggie. She opened the front door. The little apartment was toasty.

Amalia plopped onto the couch. "You climb the stairs, slowly, every day. I thought it was just a thing. It is not pride or anything. What gives?"

Maggie sat next to her. "I play sports in PE, but quit when I am tired. Or when I hurt, when my medication isn't helping."

"You, hurt? You're seventeen! Not an old lady."

"That's why we're here in Grantville. The medical care is better here." Maggie seemed to look into Amalia's soul, hesitating. "I have juvenile rheumatoid arthritis. There is no cure, but there are medications and so on."

Amalia felt like she'd been smacked in the face. Living here was hurting Maggie. "Say you will be all right. Say it."

"I am fine," Maggie insisted. "The stairs are sometimes a challenge."

An idea dawned on Amalia. Looking around the apartment, it was obvious that it wouldn't work for someone with a broken leg. The spaces between the furniture were too narrow for someone on crutches and worse for a wheelchair. The deep bathtub was a hazard, the toilet the wrong height. Not to mention how steep the stairs were. It was an obstacle course.

Amalia blinked. "What if, what if my family comes home?"

"This weather is bad," agreed Maggie.

"It is. But, but. It won't work. The apartment doesn't work." Amalia said, "We need a new house."

"Oh, I hadn't considered...I think you're right," Maggie said. "But Grantville has a housing crunch. There's not enough to go around. Never has been."

The front door opened, and Hummel came in, trailed by a carry-out boy from the food market on Main Street.

"Welcome home," Hummel said in German, continuing in accented English, "I made a quick trip out as they had brined cod for sale, and the market had preserved lemons. And I also was able to buy a dozen oranges! We are having sausages and sauerkraut for dinner." She frowned at them and asked, "What's wrong? Is it your brother?"

"It is the housing situation," Amalia said. "The apartment won't be good for Heinrich when he gets out of the hospital. My parents can't be here to fix this. So I need to fix this for them."

"We still have some time. Let me see what I can do." Hummel looked thoughtful.

Maggie interjected, "Before he became a teacher, my father did real estate here. He'll be in school tomorrow. You could ask him. I don't think he'd mind."

"Hummel, I will need to see my aunt tomorrow." Amalia said, "And Maggie, my friend, I am going to need your help tomorrow."

"I shall make the arrangements," Hummel said.

"Of course." Maggie grinned.

Amalia got up from the sofa and moved over to the big overstuffed chair by the window. The view out the window was of a darkening winter sky. On the window ledge was A Christmas Carol by Charles Dickens, the little book she'd been reading but didn't finish.

Amalia reached for it, accidentally tipping it over. She picked it up off the floor. The book fell open. The first thing she saw was, "Reflect upon your present blessings—of which every man has many—not on your past misfortunes, of which all men have some."

It took a moment to realize what it meant.

Amalia smiled to herself. It was up to her to get things moving.

One Night Only

Michael Lockwood

Magdeburg Opera House
December 24, 1635

Gunther Wagner nervously popped his knuckles as he paced behind a dropped curtain. On the other side of the curtain, a mindless buzz droned from the audience as they made their way to their seats. He pulled the curtain open just enough to catch sight of the crowd. They weren't the normal rarified gentry that these marbled walls were accustomed to. These were the poor. These were the ones who, in any other circumstances, would never have dreamed of attending an event at the Opera House.

The sight of those people made Wagner smile. For one night, they could look at themselves as something more than the dirty underclass they were. Dirty nails poked from beneath lace, and faces and necks scrubbed red popped from the neck of clean linen. Try as they might, no amount of washing or scrubbing was ever going to clean away the good, honest filth from long days in the factories.

"You should relax, Gunther," a voice drew him back from the curtains. Ortholph Fomann stood just inside the doorway, his hands cradled in front of him.

"Ortholph," he replied, "I am perfectly at ease..."

He trailed off as Fomann looked pointedly at his hands. The sound of a popping knuckle seemed to emphasize Fomann's point.

Gunther quickly dropped his hands and then stuffed them firmly into his up-timer-style woolen trousers to avoid further mischief.

"That's better," Fomann smiled. "Still, you shouldn't fret so much. Your last few rehearsals have been almost flawless."

"Almost," Wagner stressed. Ortholph Fomann smiled.

Wagner knew he had a tendency of being what the up-timers called "high strung." Wagner preferred to think of his being properly conscientious about the details around him.

"In all seriousness, Gunther, you have done well with the group."

"Thank you, Ortholph," Wagner said. "And your idea was a brilliant one."

Fomann bowed, acknowledging the compliment.

The idea for the charity event had been Fomann's idea, hatched when he and Wagner sat in the Grantville Library, comparing Christmas music that the library kept as part of its collection of music CDs against what they were used to. Wagner had found himself drawn to the a cappella carols, such as "O Holy Night" and "Mary, Did You Know?" Fomann had suggested that Wagner get a group together to sing these songs. And while Wagner was at it, why not sing for an audience?

How Fomann had gone from an audience to a charity concert, while serving as attorney general of the State of Thuringia-Franconia, was something of a blur. His friend had a knack for dizzyingly rapid trains of thought. Though, at times, Fomann's sheer magnetism tended to brush aside the intervening steps and make you wish to follow his mind where it led.

The original plan had been to hold the event in Grantville (Wagner had noticed that Fomann had already assumed that Wagner would form the group). However, it was dismissed after due consideration. For all of its wealth, the individuals were rarely wealthy enough to afford what Fomann had in mind. They were also wiser and far too practical for an endeavor like this. Nor did they have a venue for something like this. The Thuringen Gardens was an outstanding place and would have welcomed the concert. But, as the idea grew, they needed something far grander.

That left one possibility, Magdeburg. The imperial city was a bustling industrial town, with all the wealth that implied. And being the center of government for the United States of Europe, the city tended to be swarmed by *adel* of all types. Indeed, there had been enough wealth that Mary Simpson, the "Dame of Magdeburg," had been able to raise the contributions needed to build the Magdeburg Opera House itself.

On Christmas Eve, those same contributors were likely at parties reserved for similarly wealthy elites.

But the poor didn't have that option. There were few parties, and those tended to be somber affairs. They weren't destitute, but the wages, even as Magdeburg's economy roared along, were still small in comparison.

Fomann had enlisted the help of the Magdeburg Committee of Correspondence to pick the recipients of those donations. While Fomann could have put together a process to award those donations, the CoC had the pulse of the public and knew where the need was greatest.

Wagner set those considerations aside. They were items that Fomann addressed, not one Gunther Wagner. Instead, he turned to the other aspect of this endeavor, the entertainment. The hardest part of his part was deciding on which songs to include and which to not. Fomann had wanted something that combined up-time and down-time but kept it relatable.

The first thing Wagner had done was to eliminate any of the carols which held no religious significance. That meant that Frosty and Rudolph were ejected, to Ortholph's histrionic dismay. Any song with a Santa Claus character would be confusing. The up-timers' Santa figure was a mishmash of so many legends and traditions that it would be almost impossible to craft a "Santa" that wouldn't confuse half the audience.

Fomann had suggested "Grown Up Christmas List," which was one of Leah's favorites. However, the song felt unrealistic. There would always be wars, and lives would always be torn apart. It was simply a fact of life. As inevitable as the sunrise or death itself. The sentiment was beautiful, but, for Germans living in this world, the lyrics would come across as inane and false.

Next, Wagner needed to translate up-timer English to Amideutsch and make reference changes to things that down-timers understood. This had killed a few other songs from their list. Wagner had wanted to include "Grandma Got Run Over by a Reindeer." It was a hilarious song, one that had humor that this audience would appreciate, but there were simply too many up-timer references that would either lose the audience or ruin the sense of the song.

His group was a solid one, in his opinion. Each one had earned their place in the troupe by satisfying even Wagner's high, one might say insanely high, standards. There were six of them, including Wagner himself. One bass, two baritones, a tenor, a contralto, and a soprano. He took a moment to review their program for tonight. It was only ten songs, about an hour or so of songs. They couldn't be too long with it. Many had other obligations to attend to, such as the Catholic Christmas Mass to celebrate. They didn't want to eat into the time they needed to devote to their faith or their families.

David Sherwood was one of their baritones, Wagner was the other. However, he was also a mimic in the flesh, and his ability to recreate sounds was frankly stupendous. His "solo" was more of a glorified skit than a song. During the research for this concert, he had discovered an up-time English comedian named Rowan Atkinson. David was particularly inspired by a skit of a janitor having discovered an invisible drum set.

In many ways, it was a perfect icebreaker. The audience currently finding their seats were undoubtedly apprehensive of what the event would entail. The Opera House had a reputation for only the most talented and upper-classed entertainment. However, these people would have been bored into numbness by any operetta in Italian. On the other hand, they had no compunction about physical comedy that the upper-class would probably find beneath them. David's skit would relax them, unless Wagner was sorely mistaken.

Their bassist would follow. Randolph Klausmann could rumble the leaves off the trees if he had a mind to. It was a deep, velvety bass that seemed perfectly appropriate from such a large man. He had a ready smile and a lively sense of humor. He also had a stereotypical ruddy complexion that tended towards extremes when the weather became colder. It was notable enough that David had jokingly called him "Randolph the Red-Nosed Bassist." Randolph had thought it was hilarious and had begun wearing a ridiculous headset of brown felt antlers to their practices. Between him and David, they both kept the group smiling and morale high.

Randolph had chosen "Little Drummer Boy." He liked the simplicity of the song and that it gave him and David a chance to work together. He and David would start the song alone, Randolph singing and David performing the "drum" accompaniment. The remainder of the troupe would join with the traditional, at least the up-time traditional, "BA-Rummpapa Pummm."

Leah Rosano would follow with her solo. Her contralto voice was on the high end of that range, almost into the mezzo-soprano. In an absolute pinch, she could double as a second soprano, though her voice didn't have the timbre to make it full and rich. She once said that if she wanted to be the focus of an audience's attention, she would have trained for soprano. She was happy with her normal supplemental backup vocals.

She had initially balked at the idea of having a lead role in a song of her choice. She wasn't shy, per se. She simply didn't wish to be defined by a role. She wanted to be able to explore any range, any piece that interested her rather than to be expected to be "the soprano." Only after a lot of pressure had she agreed. Indeed, she had surprised them in both her song choice and the role. Her choice was "Amazing Grace," and she wasn't simply going to lead. She was going to solo. That was the condition of her stepping into the fore.

It was true that it wasn't a Christmas song or carol, but there had been no disagreement with her choice. It was a song meant to praise the Lord. It was beautiful in its simplicity and sincerity. What more could you ask from any song on a day to celebrate Jesus and the gospel that he brought to this world? The up-timers could keep their "Frosty the Snowman" or their "Grandma Got Run Over By A Reindeer." Christmas was faith, friends, and family.

Wagner would follow with his lead, "Mary, Did You Know?" His voice was a dead center baritone, almost perfect for this song. There were a few places where he would have to reach for the correct notes, but not too many. David was going to add some percussional accompaniment and Randolph would follow Wagner's lead on how to bring his bass in. Leah and Morgan, their soprano, had worked a quiet harmony.

The next song was one the entire group had fallen in love with immediately upon hearing it. "How Great Thou Art" was another gospel rather than Christmas song. But, like "Amazing Grace," it was simply too beautiful to pass up, tears had welled in Randolph's eyes, and Wagner wasn't ashamed to admit he felt a little sting in his as well. The great bass had requested that he be able to open the song. He knew exactly how he wanted to do it. Johann, their tenor, and Morgan had composed a kind of canticle, or over melody, that would softly interweave through the main lyrics.

The song elicited visions of majesty and grandeur. Randolph had commented once that when he closed his eyes, he saw snow-capped mountains and verdant valleys stretching before him. For Wagner, it was as though his mind tried to flood itself with all of God's magnificent works, to take in all the beauty the Lord had created and try to understand the very fabric of creation. He knew he failed each time he did that, but the sense of awe that he felt each time he sang this song, especially with the troupe, made him want to try again.

"What Child Is This?" was an interesting song. The base melody was a known, and relatively popular English tune called "Greensleeves." However, the Christmas lyrics wouldn't be written until something like two and a half centuries later. Fomann had insisted they include it in their program. It was the embodiment of what he was trying to achieve, finding a way to bring down-time and up-time cultures into harmony, no pun intended.

None of the troupe had any problems with it, after all, the charity event was called *Carols of Christmas Future* after all. Fomann had thought the name ridiculous until Wagner had reminded him that the idea of convincing pampered *adel* to loan some of their worn-out finery to the peasantry. Sumptuary laws, and more importantly *adel* egos, had to be observed. Tonight's audience was dressed in the manner expected for the

Opera House without the borrowed clothing breaking those laws. No *adel* would ever wear these outfits again, not after one of the rabble had worn it, but "lending" it to the event let them skirt, officially at least, the laws and egos. The clothes, once returned, would be remade into draperies or similarly recycled.

Wagner brought himself back to his task, making sure their performance was worth the effort. He would let others worry about the sheer waste and debauchery of so many fine silks and other valuable cloth, not to mention the hours of labor from seamstresses.

Morgan LeBlanc would follow with her soprano singing "Ave Maria." In one way, the song was a nod to the Catholics in the audience. In another, it was Morgan's favorite song. The song could be performed in multiple tempos, but she had found a version performed by an up-timer soprano named Sarah Brightman that was on the slower side. Morgan planned on changing a few things, adding some runs and altering a few pieces of phrasing.

Morgan wasn't a diva, but she did like to show off her talents. The collection in which she had found "Ave Maria" also held a recording of an opera written by a composer named Mozart. The opera, *The Magic Flute*, had an aria in it, known as "The Aria of the Night Queen." It required a very quick, very light *coloratura* and was well outside Morgan's *tessitura*, her comfortable vocal range. She knew it was, and it wasn't a song she would sing for a performance, but for practice and preparing for a performance. She said it quickened her ability to change note shifts and cycle through the range that she was comfortable with.

"O Holy Night" was special. Their tenor, Johann Grossmann, was another natural, though he lacked the self-confidence that the others had. He was a quiet, mouselike man who rarely spoke and generally tried to blend into the background of any room he could. Both David and Randolph were doing their best to bring Johann out of his shell, so to speak. However, the closest thing to a victory they had achieved was getting Johann very drunk and very hungover.

But that shy, timid man disappeared once he opened his mouth in song. Randolph had once said that he finally understood how angels must sound in heaven above. Wagner, for his part, could only agree. Germans didn't have a tradition of fae and fairies, but he was sure any pagan from the English Isles would swear Grossmann gained his voice from the Seelie Court.

The next song was the one that Wagner was most excited about, "Christmas Canon." The first of many reasons is that it was simply a beautiful song. The words were simple but all the more beautiful for their simplicity.

A canon was simply a piece of music that had multiple melodies being performed at the same time. "Row, Row, Row Your Boat" was an example when each voice starts off with the initial leader line and the next voice begins after the first iteration. Altogether, the result was an intermingling of seemingly chaotic sounds that tickled the ear.

However, more importantly, Wagner was excited because he and Fomann had a surprise for their audience. They had worked with the Committees of Correspondence and the schools for the last few months coming up with creative ways to sneak each attendee's child to singing practice. There were only three lines of vocals. Each child only had to learn one line for their part. After that, it was about learning timing and avoiding distractions against losing your place. And if you did, you just picked up, no harm. A few of the older ones would assist the troupe with the underlying melody that was usually performed by a set of violins.

They had practiced in small groups more often than not and they were able to practice as a whole about six times in the last few months. It wasn't in tune. It was ragged. It wasn't even remotely polished.

But it was beautiful. There was something about children singing that warmed almost any heart, even one as finicky as one Gunther Wagner. The children enjoyed keeping a surprise from their parents, and it seemed like the vast majority actually did. The event was about enjoying a night of something special. Whether it was dressing in fine clothes and the opera or actually singing in the opera, Wagner hoped it was a memory that they all cherished.

The final song was "Auld Lang Syne." Wagner had placed this at the end of their night's performance. It was a traditional song from the up-timers' universe that was sung for the transition from December 31st to January 1st, at the stroke of midnight. Wagner felt it was appropriate as the closing song with one that closed out one year for another. Unlike "Grown Up Christmas List," which asked for impossible things, "Auld Lang Syne" begged the listener to remember the good of the years passed and pull them into the new.

Ortholph Fomann clapped his hands for attention.

"Attention all! Attention!" Fomann motioned for the singers to gather around. "This is an amazing night! You have worked hard and have my admiration and respect. I'm sure each and every man, woman, and child will look back upon this night and smile for years to come."

He paused and looked each of them in the eye, letting them see his warm affection.

"For one night, they are *adel*."

With that, Wagner cleared his throat and pulled out his pitch pipe.

"It's one night only,"—he raised the pipe to his mouth—"so let's make it one to remember."

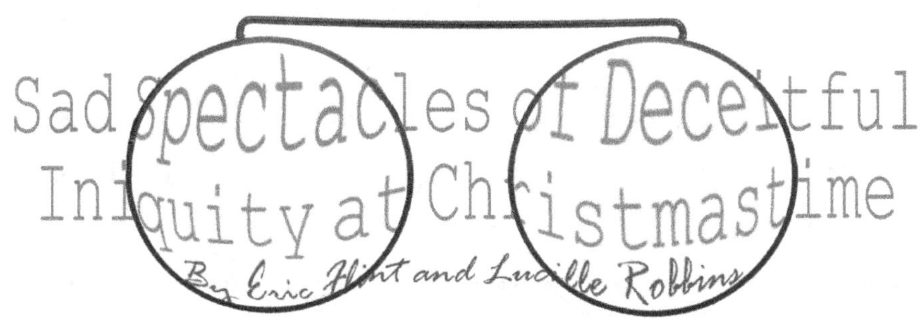

Sad Spectacles of Deceitful Iniquity at Christmastime

Eric Flint and Lucille Robbins

Nuremberg

Nadler's Apothecary

November 21, 1637

Hearing the bell on the door of his apothecary ring, Ulrich Nadler came out of the workroom to see who had entered. He was still working the pestle in the mortar because the concoction he was making took a lot of grinding, and he knew from experience that it was too easy to find excuses to break off the tedious labor.

"Ah, Kuntz." Still working the mortar and pestle, he used both hands to indicate a small table in the corner of the apothecary's showroom. "Have a seat. I'll be with you in just a few minutes."

Looking gloomy as he so often did, Kuntz Pauerschmidt took off his heavy coat, brushed off a light dusting of snow, and hung it on a coatrack near the door. His wide-brimmed hat went on the same peg, after which he moved to the table and sat down. He said nothing further; just stared out the front window of the apothecary onto the street beyond. The window was more like a panel of small diamond-shaped glass panes than what the American up-timers called a "window," being the insufferable braggarts that they were.

Once he was back in the workroom, Ulrich said to his wife Agnes, "Kuntz dropped by for a visit."

"Oh, joy," she said.

He smiled. "Be nice—charitable, at any rate. He's an unhappy man these days."

"He's an unhappy man each and every day. I remember him as a boy. Even then, Kuntz could find a worm in every apple. What will it be this time?"

"The foul machinations of Georg Schwanhardt, I imagine. He's been obsessive about the man lately."

Agnes finished grinding her own concoction and poured the fine powder into a jar. "The glass engraver?" she asked, frowning. "What's he care about him?"

"He's convinced that Schwanhardt has designs on the spectacle makers guild."

Agnes rolled her eyes. "Kuntz has been convinced that somebody has wicked designs on his guild since he was an apprentice. There's a new word in Amideutsch for the weird way his mind works. Something like 'paranormal.' "

"Paranoid," her husband supplied. "Seeing enemies everywhere." He smiled again. "Of course, just because you have imaginary enemies doesn't mean you don't have real ones too."

"A glass engraver? Schwanhardt's not even a lens maker. I've never seen his work, but from what I hear he makes finely etched goblets."

Ulrich nodded. "So he does. I have seen one of his pieces. Beautiful work. Mostly miniature landscapes."

He finally finished his grinding, and, as Agnes had done earlier, poured the substance into a jar. And, just as she has done, was careful to put a label on it. Most of what an apothecary produced took the form of fine white powder. If you didn't label it right away, you were likely to forget what was in the jar. And you did *not* want to have to taste it to find out.

"We'll do well in the upcoming Christmas market," said Agnes, stripping off her gloves and wiping her brow with a cloth. "But I won't be sorry to be done with all the extra work."

Ulrich managed to shrug while stripping off his own gloves. "What else can you do? Our city's Christmas market is one of the oldest, probably the biggest, and certainly the most famous one in the Germanies. In the few weeks it lasts, we get more than one-third of our yearly income from it."

That was true enough. It always surprised Agnes a little, since Christmas markets were mostly associated with the sale of foodstuffs and decorations. But every year they closed down their shop and set up a booth in the *Hauptmarkt*, the central square in Nuremberg's old town which was the heart of the Christmas market. The sheer scale of the traffic guaranteed excellent sales of their goods.

"All right, let's go see what has Kuntz upset now," said Ulrich, heading for the showroom.

"Do I have to?" muttered Agnes. But she followed him out of the workroom. Kuntz Pauerschmidt occupied the position of an exasperating but very old friend, the sort of person you just didn't treat badly. It helped that for all his lamentations and grousing, he was reliable when you needed him and was always kind toward their children.

* * *

"So what has you in a foul mood today?" asked Ulrich, as he and Agnes took seats at the same table.

"It's that Czech bastard," said Kuntz. "He's up to no good again. I know he is. I just can't prove it yet."

"Schwanhardt? He's not Czech, he's German."

"Born and bred right here in Nuremberg," Agnes added.

"Doesn't matter." Pauerschmidt waved his hand dismissively. "He spent years in Prague, studying under that rat bastard, Caspar Lehmann."

"Who was also German," said Agnes. She didn't bother inquiring as to the reason Kuntz considered the man a "rat bastard." First, because he was sure to have a reason—or several. Second, because he would go on at length on the subject. And third, because his complaints were sure to be petty.

"He spent too many years in Prague," insisted Kuntz. "He's infected with Bohemian immorality. Treachery and double-dealing are second nature to those folk." He wagged his finger in admonition. "You watch! He wants to undermine the spectacle makers guild."

Nuremberg
Workshop of Georg Schwanhardt
November 22, 1637

In this particular instance, Kuntz Pauerschmidt's paranoia was justified—except that Georg Schwanhardt didn't so much want to undermine the spectacle makers guild as melt it down altogether in order to create a coherent and logically organized optical industry. He had come to regard all guilds as medieval relics—at best. They were more often a hindrance to commercial and industrial expansion than anything else.

It had to be done shrewdly, though. For whatever peculiar reason innate to human reasoning—lack thereof, rather—people clung to outdated customs, institutions and rituals all the tighter the more illogical they became.

So. This called for the use of the main-gauche as the killing weapon, after distracting one's opponent with dramatic flourishes of the rapier.

"You have your people in place?" he asked the main-gauche.

"We're getting there," replied Tommy Wayne Sloan, leaning back in his chair in the small office in Georg's workshop. Both his posture and tone of voice exuded the confident insouciance of a young man who was in fact good at what he did but had not yet encountered enough of the universe's foibles to realize that being capable was not always enough.

"I need you to define 'getting there' a bit more precisely, if you would."

Tommy brought his chair and himself upright. "The one area our progress hasn't been as much as I'd like is in organizing Augsburg's lensmakers. But I think that's just because I haven't spent much time there yet."

"I believe you're right. The lensmakers in Augsburg ought to be more partial to unionization than most skilled workers. There is no guild for lensmakers in that city, so those who don't have the wherewithal to establish their own business—which is most of them—are someone else's employees."

"That's the way I see it, too," said Tommy. "I've already got four journeymen who've been working on making the standardized lenses. We have more than three hundred stockpiled already, in all sizes from +1 to +3. Two of them have agreed to move to Nuremberg for the duration of the Christmas Market. That should be enough to fit the lenses into whatever spectacles we sell."

That was the innovation that Georg was making in lenscrafting. He'd gotten the idea from eyeglasses he'd encountered in Grantville—ones that had made it through the Ring of Fire. He thought of it as the Foster Grant method. Instead of the painstaking work of crafting lenses which suited the eyesight problems of specific people, just mass-produce standardized lenses in set gradations in terms of magnifying power.

That wasn't much use for people suffering from nearsightedness, but farsightedness was the more common problem for people as they aged—and, more the point, became more prosperous. Unless he was badly mistaken, Georg expected sales of his very fancy eyeglasses at the Christmas Market to range from splendid to spectacular. They'd still be expensive eyewear due to the embellishments and décor, but the standardized lenses would keep the price within reach of prosperous burghers. Sales wouldn't be restricted to the nobility and urban patricians.

"It seems to me you've done very well, Tommy. What has you concerned?"

"It's not the Christmas Market phase of the work, it's the later unionizing stages. Trying to get those pigheaded Augsburg lenscrafters to see themselves as workers—which is what they really are—instead of guildmasters won't be easy."

Georg shrugged. "You'll deal with that problem when the time comes. Do you have any other concerns?"

The young American labor organizer pursed his lips for a moment. Then, shook his head again. "No, not really. I'd say we're either on schedule or ahead of it—with the one exception, of course, of the spectacle makers guild right here in Nuremberg."

"That's a given," said Georg. "Those people never saw a step forward they didn't distrust and detest. To be honest, I don't think there's much chance of winning more than a handful over to us. The rest will have to be driven like hogs to the slaughter." He smiled. "Figuratively speaking, of course."

He leaned forward, planting weight upon his forearms resting on his desk. "Just remember, Tommy. We must be ready to strike no later than the last week of the Christmas Market. I am using strike in the literal sense of the term. I'm not much given to poetry."

Tommy chuckled. "No, you sure aren't."

* * *

After Tommy left, Georg turned his attention to the next stage of his plot. The first flourish of the rapier, as it were. To that end, he sent a short message to the heads of all the guilds in Nuremberg who were relevant to his purpose.

> *I have no desire to stir up animosities or cause problems for any guild in the city. I have a proposal which I believe will satisfy all parties involved in the current controversy. Let us schedule a meeting at the Rathaus as soon as possible. I leave it to the spectacle makers guild to set a time for the gathering.*
>
> *Georg Schwanhardt, Nuremberg School of Engravers*

In many cities in Germany, perhaps even most of them, the council of guilds would have just squashed his attempted intervention in fiercely-protected guild affairs. But the guilds in Nuremberg were too weak to do that.

To begin with, the city had no council of guilds. That was because in 1349, almost three centuries earlier, the guilds had rebelled against the domination of the patrician class over Nuremberg's affairs, in the so-called "Craftsmen's Uprising." The patricians won a decisive victory and stripped the guilds of any political power. The guilds remained, but henceforth their activities were restricted to purely commercial affairs. That made them much weaker than the guilds typically were in German cities.

Nuremberg
Ratskeller in the Rathaus
November 31, 1637

It took a week to get an agreement as to a meeting time—which was faster than guilds normally did anything. Georg was not concerned, however. He still had more than three weeks to carry off his coup de main.

When the meeting did finally begin, it was neither on time nor well-organized. But Georg did not fret over that, either, since he expected it from long experience. For reasons lost in the mists of time, the optical guilds had emerged from the brewers guilds and retained in full measure one of the traditions of their ancestry. Alcoholic beverages were consumed early and readily—which was not the least of the reasons the meetings were invariably held in a city's Rathaus. Georg himself was hardly what anyone would call abstemious, but in this milieu he was considered a borderline ascetic.

Nuremberg's Rathaus, or town hall, like most in the Germanies, had a tavern in the basement known as the Ratskeller—"council's cellar"—which was where the meeting was being held. As usual, for any time of day or night, the lighting in the Ratskeller was dim. Georg took advantage of that to study the other men gathered at the big table in the center of the room without being too obvious about it.

Kuntz Pauerschmidt, one of the luminaries—usually the term loosely—of the spectacle makers guild, was looking his usual gloomy self. Sitting next to him, the master of his guild, Reitz Mohn, had a much cheerier countenance, as he usually did once he'd downed a couple of steins of beer. The same was true of most of the guildsmen gathered at the table.

Georg decided the time was propitious. He stood up and raised his stein, calling for a toast to the city's Christmas market, which had opened a few days earlier and was now entering its full splendor and glory.

Once the toast was drunk, Georg brought his now-empty stein down on the table in a gesture so firm and dramatic that it bordered on slamming it down.

"An announcement! Our newly formed decorative eyeglass guild has no desire to encroach on the territory of the established guilds, certainly not"—here he gave a small bow to Guildmaster Mohn—"the venerable spectacle makers guild. Our product is intended only for frivolous entertainment, nothing more." Now he gave a small bow to the Italian lensmakers in the cellar. "And it would of course be pointless for us to encroach on the work of making lenses. Everyone here knows that lenses have to be tailor-made to serve the specific eyesight needs of each individual customer."

He grinned. "Those who would be entertained by our spectacles will have to take their chances walking down stairs, negotiating their way through the throngs at soirees and revels, and spotting awkwardly placed spouses in time to sidle away with their mistresses and courtesans."

A great laugh erupted in the cellar. Further toasts were made, in which all joined in except Kuntz Pauerschmidt, who now looked downright morose.

"I warn you, Guildmaster," he hissed to Mohn after he resumed his seat following yet another toast, "the Bohemian swine is up something."

Mohn ignored him. Kuntz could grow tiresome, and what harm could there be in the production of eyeglasses so loaded down with fripperies they could not possibly compete with the stout and sturdy products of his own guild? Especially since the spectacle makers guild had excellent relations with the Italian lenscrafter guild who would have to supply any lenses for Schwanhardt's frivolities. Say better, follies.

Nuremberg
Hauptmarkt (Central Square)
December 4, 1637

"Look! There's another one!" exclaimed Agnes. She reoriented her husband by tugging on his elbow and pointing toward a woman standing at a pastry booth ten yards away. Since Agnes was pointing with a tankard of glühwein in her hand, the gesture wasn't particularly noticeable, so she wasn't afraid of being considered rude. The bespectacled woman herself didn't spot it because she was engrossed in choosing which pastry she wanted. Her choice seemed to have narrowed down to stollen or marzipan.

Ulrich Nadler contemplated the spectacles his wife had pointed out, drinking from his own tankard as he did so. He took his time about it. Glühwein was a traditional German drink for the season and needed to be savored. Basically, it was a variety of mulled wine, which was popular all over central Europe and Scandinavia during the winter.

The spectacles were...well, a spectacle in their own right. At the core were the usual round-lensed frames, except these had a simple nose bridge instead of the traditional nose-clamp—what the French called pince-nez—and relied on side-pieces that rested atop the earlobes to hold and stabilize the eyeglasses. If Ulrich remembered what he'd been told correctly, those side pieces were called "temples."

The design was also known as "the American style." Ulrich had heard that from his friend Kuntz, who had practically spit out the words. "As if there was anything wrong with our methods and customs!" he'd added.

Wanting to keep the peace, Ulrich hadn't said anything. But he'd tried on the traditional frames made by the spectacle makers guild and found them extremely uncomfortable. The nose clamp had to be tight or the eyeglasses would just fall off. And no matter how tight you made the clamp short of actually drawing blood, the spectacles *still* fell off fairly regularly. Some people took to stabilizing the spectacles with a handheld side brace, but most just kept their heads tipped back—which was also uncomfortable.

Ulrich hadn't yet tried on a pair of spectacles "in the American style," but they certainly looked more stable and comfortable.

There was no way the traditional nose-clamp method could have supported the spectacles the woman at the pastry booth was wearing. Perched above the glasses were ascending circular medallions made of filigreed silver, topped with a crossbar that looked like engraved glass held in place with more silver filigree. Descending from the temples—which seemed to be made of copper—were spirals of yet more filigreed silver holding small gems and jewels. They resembled earrings, in a way, except for their size and quite evident weight. If those spirals had been suspended from flesh earlobes instead of metal temples, they would soon have become painful.

The woman chose a stollen, paid for it, and walked away. Watching her go, Ulrich was struck by the apparent ease with which she supported the incredible contraption. She might be moving slightly slower than she normally would, but other than that she seemed to be having no trouble keeping the spectacles in place.

"Impressive," said Ulrich.

"I don't think you spotted the most impressive thing," said Agnes.

"Which was?"

"There were eyeglasses retained inside those frames. I thought they weren't supposed to have any lenses."

Ulrich lowered his tankard and tried to find the woman again. But she had vanished into the crowded and tortuous lanes of booths.

"Ha!" he said, looking around. "Where is this booth of Schwanhardt's, do you know?"

Agnes shrugged. "I have no idea. But we ought to be able to find someone who can direct us properly." She looked around herself. "Like him!" Again, she used her tankard to point to someone, in this instance a stout man who practically had well-to-do burgher tattooed on his forehead. The spectacles he was wearing were somewhat more sedate than the ones the woman at the pastry booth had worn, but they were still clearly one of Schwanhardt's products.

When questioned, he gave them directions to the Decorative Spectacles booth that were good enough that they only lost their way twice. Trying to find any specific booth in the Christmas Market when it was in full swing was a genuine challenge.

But eventually they got there. The first thing that struck them was how big the booth was. Actually, it wasn't "a" booth, it was three booths which Schwanhardt and his people had redesigned to fit together. Oddly, though, only the first booth was fully open to the public. That was the booth where the wares were displayed.

There was a big sign on the far wall of the booth, with visual displays of traditional spectacles next to it. The sign read:

STOP TORTURING YOURSELF

WITH SPECTACLES WHOSE COUSINS

ARE THE RACK AND THE IRON MAIDEN

Agnes laughed. "I hope Kuntz doesn't see that! He might have a stroke."

After questioning one of the salesmen regarding the cost of the various items on display, Ulrich said to Agnes: "All right, we can afford the simpler and more practical designs readily enough. Do you want a pair for yourself?"

She shook her head. "No—not this evening, anyway." With a sly smile: "I'll let you do the experimenting to make sure you don't grow a third eye or something of the sort."

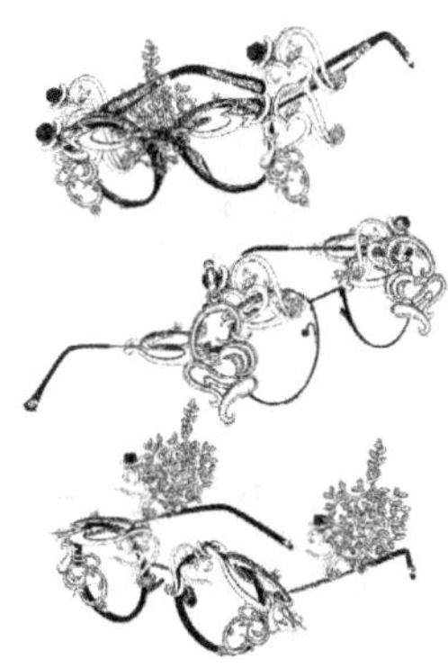

The spectacles which Merkel selected were not too far removed from traditional spectacles, at least insofar as the part of the frame which held the lenses were concerned. The differences were that it had a sturdy nose bridge which rested on the nose rather than pinching it, the "American style" temples, and—this feature was new to him—the forward part of the temples were shielded with thin copper plates. That could prove useful. It was easy to accidentally blow the fine powder of pharmaceuticals into the sides of your eyes. That was always irritating and sometimes could be painful and even dangerous.

"I'll buy them," he announced.

After the purchase was completed, the salesman ushered him to a door leading to the next booth. "They'll fit you with your lenses," the salesman announced.

When Ulrich and Agnes came into the booth, they discovered a peculiar arrangement. There was a chair in the middle of the room facing once of the walls, upon which was a bizarre chart:

G

OB

SNCU

ZKIMW

YXVQLPD

"Read the line with the smallest print you can manage," said the salesman staffing that booth.

Ulrich managed to get all but one letter in the fourth line correct. (He mistook the K for an R.)

The salesman jotted something down on a slip of paper and handed it to Ulrich. "Give this to one of the fellows in the next booth."

Passing through that door, Ulrich and Agnes found themselves in a booth where two men sat at a long table, which held boxes containing various lenses and implements which Ulrich took to be the tools of the lenscrafters' trade.

Lens fitters, rather. Ulrich handed the slip from the eyesight tester to one of the men seated at the table. He glanced at it—all it said was "1.5+"—and then took two lenses out of one of the boxes. It took him very little time to fit the lenses into the empty frames and seal them in place by simply pinching a few clips.

"Here you go," he said, handing Ulrich his new spectacles.

As soon as Ulrich put them on, he was struck by two things. First, they fit quite comfortably. The triple rest and stabilization provided by the nose bridge and the two earpieces took a little getting used to, but they were a far easier way to keep the spectacles in place than traditional frames. ("Cousins of the rack and iron maiden" was perhaps an unkind way of putting it, but the description wasn't that far off.)

Secondly, and more surprising, he could actually see better. At least, anything he was looking at up close—which was what his trade mostly required.

"You should get yourself a pair," he told Agnes.

She shook her head. "It's too soon to tell if you're growing a third eye."

* * *

Kuntz Pauerschmidt came by the apothecary for a visit two days later, but he wound up not staying long.

The moment he spotted the new spectacles on Ulrich's face, he shrieked "*How could you?*" Then, rushed out of the apothecary, slamming the door behind him.

Georg Schwanhardt's new manufactory

Nuremberg

December 16, 1637

At lunchtime, Georg called a halt to the bustling labor inside his brand-new manufactory and summoned all his employees to a meeting in the cafeteria. For some of the employees, especially the lower-skilled ones, this was the first time they'd ever entered the cafeteria. They still weren't used to the idea that an employer would provide his workers with a free breakfast and lunch.

But there were a lot of things some of them were still getting used to—first and foremost, the fact that they now belonged to a trade union. About half of them had no clear idea what a trade union was in the first place.

Once all of them were seated, Georg rose from his chair and gestured toward the two other men seated at his table. One of them was known by almost all of them because he'd been the man who organized them in the first place: the young up-timer Tommy Wayne Sloan. The other was a stranger to most of the employees. He was a man in early middle age, somewhere in his forties. From various subtle features of his dress and demeanor—nor to mention his teeth—they all knew he was a down-timer.

"Let me introduce to you Wolfgang Behringer. He is one of the vice-presidents of the International Glass Workers Union, and is the interim president of Local Union 43." Georg made a little twirling motion with his forefinger. "Local 43 is you people."

He resumed his seat, gesturing toward Behringer once again. "He will now address you."

Behringer rose and cleared his throat. "This is a somewhat unusual situation, because—this almost never happens, trust me—your employer Georg Schwanhardt has been very cooperative with the union." He cleared his throat again. "As a rule, the union's relationship with management is, ah, not congenial."

Another clearing of the throat. "That lack of congeniality normally produces a protracted period wherein the union organizes itself, usually goes out on strike"—here he rolled his hand over a couple of times—"and so on and so forth. That gives the members of the union time to get to know each other, which eventually leads to the leaders of the local union being chosen by an election."

He held up his hand rigidly. "I assure you! That same approach will be applied here as well. But we needed to move very swiftly, because one of the conditions of the management of Universal Optics was that we had to negotiate a contract very quickly. So we had no choice but to organize everything from the top down."

"What is Universal Optics?" asked one of the workers.

"This is," said Georg, again making that twirling motion with his finger. "Me, you, my foremen and salesmen, the janitors, everyone who works here."

That announcement obviously came as a surprise to most of them. Accustomed to the mores of the time, they thought of "employers" as specific people, not institutions.

"And are all those people in the union?" asked the same worker.

"Certainly not!" said Wolfgang, sounding quite indignant. "Management—that includes the foremen and well as the proprietor—is never part of the union! They are...well..." He cleared his throat again. "The enemy of labor. As a rule."

Georg smiled congenially. "I hope to maintain a much friendlier spirit here in Universal Optics. But, no, no one who has disciplinary authority will belong to the union. That would undermine the very purpose of a union. Not will certain employees whose skills and work are of a technical nature. My two bookkeepers, for instance, will not be members of the union."

"To get back to the point of this meeting," said Wolfgang, "we need to vote on the contract which we've worked out with management." His expression now seemed to combine satisfaction, surprise, and perhaps a bit of embarrassment.

He began passing out small sheafs of paper bound together with paper clips. "This is the full language of the contract. I will summarize the main provisions. You are already familiar with the wages offered, of course."

That produced a lot of smiles and not a few outright grins. Universal Optics was paying better wages for every trade involved in the business. Much better, in many cases.

What followed caused the smiles and grins to be replaced for the most part with frowns and blank expressions. That was not because anyone was hostile to the various proposals but simply because the concepts were often unclear.

One week of paid vacation after one year of service.
Two weeks after five years of service.

"What is a 'vacation'?" asked one employee.

Five days paid sick leave per year.

"What is 'sick leave'?" asked another employee.

In the event of disciplinary action being taken against an employee, said employee has the right to appeal. A joint committee of union representatives and foremen will adjudicate the appeal. If no agreement can be reached, the dispute will be turned over to a neutral arbitrator acceptable to both parties to decide.

It went on for quite some time. There were a lot of questions.

One of the lenscrafters, either because he was bolder than the others or because he'd had more contact with up-timers, asked the question: "What about medical insurance?"

"I'm afraid that's not possible," said Georg, "for the simple reason that there are as yet no medical insurance companies that deal with anyone except wealthy individuals. But we will set up a medical fund to provide as much assistance as possible."

"We don't want employer-based medical insurance anyway," growled Wolfgang. "That's what the up-timers had where they came from, and it had far too many problems. The unions are pushing the legislatures in the USE to set up some kind of state-subsidized medical insurance."

"Nuremberg isn't part of the USE," someone pointed out.

"Yes, I know," said Wolfgang. "But if we can get such provisions established in the USE"—here he smiled thinly—"I think the authorities in Nuremberg will see reason soon enough."

That produced a little laugh from several people. Nuremberg was officially a free imperial city, with complete political independence. It was also completely surrounded by the far larger and more powerful United States of Europe. Nobody—certainly not the patricians who dominated the city's political affairs—had any doubt that if the USE chose to do so, it could swallow Nuremberg without much more effort than a burp. The city maintained its independence partly because Gustav Adolf thought forbearance had general political value to him, partly because there were certain financial and commercial advantages, partly because Nuremberg provided a handy place where political refugees could take shelter under USE protection without that being formally established, and partly because Nuremberg's powers-that-be had far more sense than a goose.

* * *

Eventually, the presentation was done, all questions answered as far as they could be, and the member of IGWU Local 43 took a vote. The contract was approved unanimously.

After everyone went back to work, Tommy rose from his chair. He hadn't said a word throughout the meeting. "When do you want to start the strike?" he asked. The question was officially addressed to Wolfgang, even though Georg was a secret partner in the enterprise.

Wolfgang consulted his pocket watch. It was down-time-made to an up-time design and could maintain accurate time within five minutes for a day. "It's too late to start now," he asked. "We want to use what's left of the afternoon and evening to make our final preparations anyway. So, let's start the walkouts at 8:00 o'clock tomorrow morning."

"You got it," said Tommy, heading for the manufactory's entrance. The building was located about midway between the *Hauptmarkt* and the *Rathausplatz*. Nicely located for the purposes of the moment, and never mind that Georg Schwanhardt would insist that thought had never crossed his mind when he selected the location.

After Tommy left, Wolfgang chuckled and said, "You know, the up-timers have a name for this. A 'sweetheart contract,' they call it. Except this one is standing on its head. Your normal sweetheart contract is where the union officials give the company a contract very favorable to them—screw the employees—in exchange for which they are bribed in one way or another. But you!" He chuckled again. "You gave the union what's probably the best contract anywhere in Europe and didn't ask for anything in return. I didn't have to try to bribe you either."

"You couldn't have," said Georg, folding his hands complacently over his belly. "After the booming sales we're been having at the Christmas Market—which still has a week to run—I'm quite sure I'm much richer than you are."

Now, Wolfgang laughed outright. "I don't doubt that!" He gave George a quizzical look. "You do understand this honeymoon period—that's another up-time expression—won't last?"

"Oh, certainly. This contract will last for three years. I don't expect the next one to be much more difficult to negotiate. After that..." He pursed his lips thoughtfully. "Six years from now, by my estimate, we will start having contract negotiations that are a lot less friendly. But it doesn't matter, because by then I will have accomplished my goals."

"Which are?"

The guilds will be effectively destroyed—not just those I deal with but the whole miserable be-damned guild system in Nuremberg. I've already created a fully-rounded optical company here. We have everything under one roof, or at least guided from under one roof. We make the lenses, the frames, train lots of opticians to fit people properly with spectacles, send salesmen far and wide. Within a few years, I even hope we can help create a serious medical profession specializing in eyesight. The up-timers have a name for them, you know—ophthalmologists and optometrists, they're called."

Now he grinned. "I will have competitors, of course. Not all the guildmasters are as obtuse and pigheaded as Kuntz Pauerschmidt. But they'll be starting not only far behind me but suffering from some severe handicaps. They won't be able to match what I can offer my employees, which mean they will have constant labor problems where I don't—and I'll keep outgrowing them because I can hire the best men in the trades."

"So you're using this coming strike to break your competitors."

Georg grimaced. "Oh, 'break' is such a harsh word. I think of it rather as an educational project."

Nuremberg
Nadler's Apothecary
January 19, 1638

"So what can I do for you, Herr Nadler?" asked Georg Schwanhardt. He and Tommy Wayne Sloan were sitting in two of the chairs at the small table in the corner of the showroom next to the windows. Ulrich occupied one of the other two chairs.

"I wish to ask for your advice, Herr Schwanhardt."

"Please, call me Georg."

"In that case, please call me Ulrich. What I'd like to know is if your methods of...ah, let's call it organization, might be of use to me. The truth is, I am finding the apothecary guild's rules, regulations, and restrictions more and more irksome."

Agnes came over to the table with a tray laden with cups of tea. After setting it down, she took a seat herself. With four of them at the table, it was a little crowded, but there was enough room for all the cups.

"Not to mention that I have no desire to be forced to give up our business if Ulrich passes away," she said.

He smiled at her. "It's 'when,' I'm afraid, not 'if'. And, under the rules, you could always marry another apothecary to keep the business going."

"At which point it would become *his* apothecary, not mine. Besides, one husband in a lifetime is enough."

Georg looked around the showroom. "Can we see your workroom?" he then asked.

"Certainly."

When they returned to the table, Georg cocked a questioning eye at Tommy. The young American shook his head. "This is really a proprietor kind of business. I don't see where a union could play any role at all. On the other hand..."

"Yes?"

He pointed to one of the walls. "What's on the other side of that, Ulrich? From what I could see of it when we approached your business, the building next to yours seemed vacant."

Calling it *a building next to yours* was not really accurate. All the shops on this street abutted right next to each other. They were more like shops in an up-time strip mall than separate buildings.

"The upstairs isn't vacant. Old Ursula Treit lives there. The downstairs used to be her husband's haberdashery. When he died seven years ago, she just sold off all their goods and closed the business."

"So the downstairs would be available for lease?"

Ulrich frowned. "I suppose so. But why would I want to lease it?" He swept his finger around, indicating the showroom. "This is as much as Agnes and I need for our business."

"For an apothecary, yes. But not for a *drug store*."

Georg leaned back in his seat. "Ah. I think I see where you're going with this, Tommy. I saw some photographs in Grantville of an old establishment called...soda something."

"Soda fountain. We had one in Grantville although it closed before I was born." He turned to Ulrich. "What you do, see, is use your pharmacy as the anchor business. But you open a wide entrance into the building next door"—he pointed at the wall—"and in there you set up a soda fountain. That's a long counter with soda dispensers—"soda" is a type of sweet, non-alcoholic beverage—and you can add an ice cream assortment to go with it."

Georg was getting enthusiastic, his business acumen racing ahead. "That's how the big pharmacies up-time often got started. The soda fountain part of the operation would draw in customers looking for refreshments. As time passes, you start adding sales items next to the soda fountain as well as what you're selling in the apothecary."

"What sort of items?" asked Agnes.

"Start with medical stuff that doesn't need the attention of an apothecary. Aspirin, for instance. Bottles of laudanum." Tommy felt a little guilty making that suggestion—but, hey, opium was legal in the here and now.

"Ready-made bandages. Cough syrups," added Georg.

"And then you start adding non-medical stuff," said Tommy. He took off the baseball cap on his head and handed it to Agnes. "Get somebody to make a bunch of these for you. You can put whatever logo you want on them. They'll sell, trust me."

He gave the German couple a big and genuinely friendly smile. "Before you know it, you've launched this world's version of Walgreen's. Only it'll be called Nadler's."

"But..." Ulrich shook his head. "That's going to require a lot of money—which we don't have."

"Simple," said Georg. "I'll lend you what you need—with a good interest rate. But what I suggest instead is that we go into business together. I'll put up the capital needed for the expansion, while the two of you manage everything."

Ulrich and Agnes looked at each other. "We need time to think about this," said Ulrich.

"Of course," said Georg, nodding. "But don't take too long or somebody else will think of it."

He took a sip of his tea. "Others may complain, but I love the world the Americans set in motion when they arrived. As time passes, I've even come to the conclusion that the inspiration for the Ring of Fire came from...Well."

He took another sip of tea and pointed with his finger to the roof above their heads.

After a moment, Agnes grasped his meaning. "Divine intervention? Be serious, Georg! Not even the Americans make that claim."

"That's not entirely true," said Tommy. "There's an old guy in Grantville named Tino Nobili—a pharmacist, as it happens. He's, ah, the town's most famous reactionary. The standard joke about him is that he's to the right of Attila the Hun. Anyway, he's been saying for years that God sent Grantville to the seventeenth century."

Tommy drained his cup. "As punishment for our sins."

The View From Nakatomi Tower

Walt Boyes and Bjorn Hasseler

December 24, 1635

The last strains of the soundtrack played, and the credits rolled. The very old, squeaky VHS tape cassette managed to make it through another showing. Out in the auditorium, first the up-timers in the audience started to cheer, then the slightly more reserved down-timers began to clap and hoot. The credits ended, and the lights came up as the auditorium once more became the gymnasium of Grantville High School. People got up from the bleachers and stretched, collected their belongings, and headed out into the snow.

Inside the still-darkened projection booth, as the cassette started its rewind, Edgar Neustatter turned to Dan Frost, who was volunteering as the projectionist. That meant that he'd provided the tape of the movie and didn't want anybody else messing with it.

"I don't understand why this is a Christmas movie. It isn't really, is it?"

Dr. James Nichols walked into the booth just as Neustatter asked his question. His features were dark and silhouetted by the light coming in the open door. He swung the door shut and turned on the room lights. He was still dark-complected even when the lights went on. He was in his late fifties and any weight he'd put on hadn't kept him out of the action in Italy some months ago.

"Well, it didn't start out that way," Frost said. "It was an action thriller, and it just happened to get released at Christmas time. And there's a Christmas party in it."

Nichols laughed. "But Christmas doesn't really start until Hans falls from the top of Nakatomi Plaza," he said. "It is an up-time Christmas tradition!"

Connect with Eric Flint's 1632 & Beyond

We would love to hear from you here at *Eric Flint's 1632 & Beyond!* There are lots of ways to get in touch with us and we look forward to hearing from you.

Main Sites

Email: 1632Magazine@1632Magazine.com

Shop: 1632Magazine.com

Author Site: Author.1632Magazine.com

For anyone interested in writing in the 1632verse, or fans interested in more background on the series and how we keep track of everything.

Social Media

Our Facebook Group is our primary social media, but we do use the FB Page, YouTube, and Instagram accounts.

Facebook Group: The Grantville Gazette / 1632 & Beyond

YouTube: 1632andBeyond

Facebook Page: Facebook.com/t1632andBeyond

Reviews and More

Because reviews really do matter, especially for small publishers and indie authors, please take a few minutes to post a review online or wherever you find books, and don't forget to tell your friends to check us out!

You are welcome to join us on **BaensBar.net**. Most of the chatting about 1632 on the Bar is in the 1632 Tech forum. If you want to read and comment on possible future stories, check out 1632 Slush (stories) and 1632 Slush Comments on BaensBar.net.

If you are interested in writing in the 1632 universe, that's fabulous! Please visit **Author.1632Magazine.com** (QR code above) for more information.

www.ingramcontent.com/pod-product-compliance
Lightning Source LLC
Chambersburg PA
CBHW061237170626
4009CB00007B/2718

9781962398206